RUNNERLAND

RUNNERLAND

JOHN BURNS

RAINCOAST BOOKS

Vancouver

Raincoast Books gratefully acknowledges the financial support of the Province of British Columbia through the BC Arts Council and the Book Publishing Tax Credit and the Government of Canada through the Canada Council for the Arts, and the Book Publishing Industry Development Program (BPIDP).

Edited by Steven Beattie
Cover and interior design by Teresa Bubela

Library and Archives Canada Cataloguing in Publication

Burns, John, 1968-
    Runnerland / John Burns.

ISBN 13: 978-1-55192-957-6
ISBN 10: 1-55192-957-0

    I. Title.

PS8603.U738R86 2007   jC813'.6   C2006-905238-7

Library of Congress Control Number: 2006937072

Raincoast Books   *In the United States:*
9050 Shaughnessy Street   Publishers Group West
Vancouver, British Columbia   1700 Fourth Street
Canada V6P 6E5   Berkeley, California
www.raincoast.com   94710

Printed in Canada by Webcom

10 9 8 7 6 5 4 3 2 1

ONE FOR THE MONEY

CHAPTER ONE

There was nothing special about the day Peter's father died. At least not to start with. The alarm went and Peter hit snooze, hoping to pick up a dream about skipping stones across the sea. He was just finding his way back over the border into dreamland when the alarm went again, music on the radio, so he knew he'd dozed through news and sports. Peter reached over and slapped snooze a second time — and was tasting that first golden lick of sleep when the racket started back up, some lame Green Day power ballad he'd pay five bucks never to hear again. Was it his imagination or was even the radio on his case? It felt like everyone was, lately.

"All right, all right. I'm moving. Back off."

There was the daily dig for something halfway wearable. He glanced back at the clock. The numbers kept morphing. Even though they were going up instead of down, the LED display reminded him of those timers in bad action movies, the ones attached to rolls of dynamite. Only there wasn't any hero running in to snip the right wire just in time. 3 … 2 … 1 … Ka-bloom!

Peter dragged his eyes from radio to mirror, tugged on jeans and his second-favourite sweatshirt — it was blue, and he'd scrawled ATTENTIO DEFICI DISORDE in red Sharpie across the front — and tried to show his bed head who was boss. He licked his fingers a few times and managed to smoosh down the worst of his brown curls at the front, but the back was probably a horror show. *Don't even think about it*, he addressed what looked like a baby zit on his chin. Anyway, there wasn't time for anything more in the way of personal grooming. He gave the mirror a shrug and checked his teeth. His reflection stuck out its tongue in reply. Whatever. Peter was already bounding down the stairs and through the kitchen. He scooped up his corduroy jacket and waved to his parents sprawled over bagels and coffee, listening to the radio blah-blah about investments. Boring!

"Peter, honey," his mom said, looking over her shoulder at the digital readout on the stove.

"Can't stop, Mom. You don't want me to be late for the halls of learning, do you?"

She glanced at him, and seemed to really see him for the first time that morning. "Peter Samuel Weir. You're not wearing that awful sweatshirt with the neckband all frayed like that, are you? I thought I'd thrown that out!"

He cinched his jacket tighter across his chest and hunch-walked toward the door. Ellen had a habit of exaggerating, which his dad was always telling him was a charming tic, an example of her expansive personality, a subtle generosity. Jack Weir could go on forever like that. Peter took after his dad more than his mom — relaxed, forgiving. "A pushover," Ellen would sniff. "A patsy."

"You catch more clients with honey," Jack would reply. Not a philosophy every lawyer would agree with, but Jack wasn't every lawyer. Specializing in wills and probate, he ran his own firm — "micro-firm," he liked to say, "practically organic" — out of the house. As far as Peter could tell, honey was paying off okay for him, except when it came time to talk allowance ...

They weren't so bad, his mom and dad. At least they'd given in about the bus. Ever since Grade 9 started, Peter had been asking them — okay, begging them — to let him take the city bus into school on his own. It wasn't so much a safety thing. Some kids could barely cross a street without a parent escort. Not Peter. No, even with Ellen more than happy to quote intersection mortality stats, his parents had been strangely relaxed about road safety. It was more a time thing. They kept citing all the days he'd been late for pickup because "I just had to get a few things I forgot from my locker …" Well, he'd shown them who could be Mr. Responsible. Peter had the schedule down to a science. Okay, "science" was maybe an exaggeration. Some mornings on the way in — most mornings, if he was honest — he was a little behind, and then he had to skip breakfast and run a few blocks, race a stop or two. Hey, no big deal. It wasn't much in the way of excitement, but it got the day started. If only he could swing PE credits for it …

Charging out the door some days, he liked to toss a line back to his mom and dad, still slumped over their caffeine crutches: "I'm not bad. I'm just drawn that way." His mother would give this little smirk. Sometimes he just didn't get her. She was proud of him, of course. Not his grades exactly, but she let him know when she thought he'd done good. But if his folks were on *Jeopardy!* and the category was "Peter Weir's Shortcomings — Large and Small," his mom would clean up. Anyway, Jack was the one who should smirk. He was the one who'd rented his toddler *Who Framed Roger Rabbit*. Over Ellen's protestations, as she liked to point out. "Who could be too young for *Who Framed Roger Rabbit*?"

his dad would still sometimes ask, with a look of genuine amazement. "It won four Academy Awards!" The whole experience had left Peter with an awesome repertoire of obscure '80s cartoon dialogue and an embarrassing fear of weasels with guns. He could draw Baby Herman in his sleep.

On this bright, icy morning, the morning after Halloween and all the usual mayhem, the holiday called the Day of the Dead in some parts of the world, with toilet paper in the trees, pumpkin shrapnel in the gutters (and in their rose garden — his mom was going to freak!), the empty casings of Roman candles and Catherine wheels everywhere you looked, Peter tore down the sidewalk with the final grains of his innocence intact inside him. The pavement stretched ahead, drawing him onto the main artery into the city and, fingers crossed (3 ... 2 ... 1 ...), the bus.

"Hey, hot stuff," Mary-Beth Kennedy called as he pinballed down the aisle of the bus, collapsing into the seat beside her. "Trick-or-treat."

"Hm. Treat."

Mary-Beth lived behind the big private golf course where Ellen played a few mornings a week with friends. Mary-Beth was Peter's best friend, best *girl* friend, anyway.

He was always careful about the pause between those two words. It didn't matter what the kids at school said, she was a girl who was a friend, nothing more. And never would be anything more, not at the rate he was going.

She understood him better than anyone. All the fights at home, the arguments over what he was old enough for, who was allowed to come over, who wasn't, what parties were off-limits because they were hosted by "degenerates" and "juvenile delinquents" (that was Jack the lawyer), which privileges were on life support because he just wouldn't knuckle down and concentrate on his homework or his chores (that was Ellen being Ellen) — Mary-Beth heard about all this in long IM sessions after their parents were asleep. Her family was much more *supportive*, she claimed. More *nurturing*. She was like that, always precise with her words when she talked. Same with online: no LOLs, no smiley faces, no lowercase "i" when she meant I. She planned to become a writer, which maybe also explained why she was always studying people. "What does everyone think of me?" she'd ask him. "Like, when I'm not there. What do they say?" Sometimes being friends with Mary-Beth was like writing book reports about life at fourteen.

Peter yearned to tell her the truth. Not about the losers at school, stupid gossip from study hall when kids only had their books open to hide the notes they were writing each other (or soft-core manga), but about his own feelings, what *he* really thought, and had thought since Grade 8, probably longer. *This is the year*, Peter swore to himself as he gave Mary-Beth the lowdown on all the candy he'd scored the night before on a last-minute pass down his street. (Even though he'd sworn he wouldn't go out this year, that he was too old for trick-or-treating.) "Cuz, you know, it's a public service I'm doing. Seriously." *Good, she was smiling now.* "Otherwise, all the old ladies down the block just put that candy back in some cupboard and bring it out again next year." *Don't tell her you stayed up all the night before, painting your own devil's mask. Don't be the art nerd.* "All this candy that you can't even buy anymore, it all comes out and it's, like, disgusting, all waxy and old-tasting. That's enough to ruin some little kid's first Halloween night forever. Somebody's got to save Halloween. Somebody's got to spare all those little kids from waxy leftovers!"

Food was a big deal for the Kennedys, proper food, not Pizza Pops or Chinese takeout. And they never minded if Peter "dropped by" several nights a week for dinner and hours of fierce whispering in Mary-Beth's room. He'd even slept over a few times. On the downstairs futon, of course. It must have been during one of those dinners that she had told her parents — finked, he said later — about Peter's breakfast diet. It wasn't that he was neglected, he tried to explain.

Jack and Ellen just couldn't adapt to his particular morning approach. Would it kill them to have a little snack ready for liftoff? But no, the rule was breakfast at the table or no breakfast at all. It was tough love, nutrition-style, Ellen would say. "It's a human-rights violation!" Peter would yell back. "I'm phoning child services!" From that night on, Mary-Beth set off on each morning's calm stroll to the bus stop armed with the proteins and complex carbohydrates so necessary for growing boys.

"I'm not bad," he told her over muffins one morning, their blueberry scent skirling down the bus as he tore them apart. "I'm just drawn that way."

Mary-Beth, who was also in Grade 9, was pretty, in a relaxed, Gap model way. She had perfectly white teeth and this way of walking that always made Peter think she was testing the ground before she put her full weight on it. She was also taller than Peter, which wasn't hard because Peter was — depending on your source — either short or delayed. His mom said, "Why not face facts: the boy takes after my side of the family. Tall isn't the only thing in life. At least he got my cheekbones and my eyes. Those eyes will make up for a lot, dear." His dad held out more hope.

Today's before-school special was pancakes, with a sealable minitub of maple syrup that looked like it had been designed specifically to carry maple syrup onto buses.

Who comes up with these things? Peter wondered. *Some person is actually out there using some computer program to give the world a new shape of Tupperware.* The pancakes were buttermilk with a golden-brown bottom and creamy, bubbly top, and the syrup pooled across them like mahogany lava flowing down a tropical volcano. A fantasy of life on a desert island, just the two of them, overtook Peter's mind, every coconut in its own container. Peter imagined a combination of *Lost* and *Iron Chef*, starring him and Mary-Beth. He was just working on an imaginary logo for the tie-in clothing line when he realized Mary-Beth had been talking for some time. He reached for a Ziploc bag, shook out a handful of strawberry slices, and tried not to fixate on Mary-Beth's lips, which were big for her face and frosted this morning a pale sparkly pink, but to listen instead to the words they were forming.

"Did you do English? I can't *believe* we have another alternate reading. I mean, it's bad enough reading the book once, you know? I'd like to know who came up with the idea of alternate readings anyway."

Alternate readings, basically rewriting the endings of famous stories to make them "more relevant to the current reality as youth experience it," were the bane of Peter's existence. Ditto Mr. Richards in general.

He tried to talk around a moist mouthful of pancake: "I ..."

Mary-Beth's eyes widened. "You forgot? Again? Peter, sometimes I think you are the biggest airhead I've ever met. Mr. Richards is going to completely kill you! Just because you're acing art doesn't mean you can just ignore everything else!" She tossed her hair from side to side in an "I give up" way that she probably got off TV but that Peter still loved.

He shrugged and tried to adopt a tragic look. He leaned closer and whispered in a thick movie-spy accent over the bus' diesel whine: "Mahrry-Baith. Thees ees wery, wery important. Ve haff only moments. Eeff I die thees day, you make eet I get proper burial, yes? Zey vill play Neervana—"

"Peter! Kurt Cobain at your funeral? That is *so* tacky! Marilyn Manson maybe."

It was a ride like a thousand others. There would never be another like it.

Peter never did have to give his alternate reading for English. One minute he'd been drawing a snarling cheetah on his forearm with a ballpoint pen. The next, his name came squawking over the PA and he was a) busted and b) facing a whole classful of unblinking eyeballs. But Mr. Richards just sighed and flicked his pen, first at Peter, then at the door like he was fly-fishing and Peter was probably undersize but getting him off the hook was more effort than it was worth. The class was dead quiet as he stood, but the whispering started up before he'd even set foot in the hall.

When Peter got to the school office, he was surprised to see his mom sitting there beside the bulletin board where the kindergartners' missing mitts got pinned in winter. Ellen was still in her golfing outfit and that more than anything told him that something was very wrong. Mr. Patterson, the school principal, stood just inside his own office and motioned them in, then shut the door behind them. Peter rummaged through his memory for anything heinous he'd done recently. He and Frankie Mulholland had skipped PE the week before and smoked a cigarette from Frankie's dad out behind the kiddie climbers. Was that it? It couldn't be. And even though Frankie kept trying to convince him it was cool, the cigarette hadn't actually been much fun. Peter suspected they'd looked kind of pathetic.

Mr. Patterson cleared his throat. The principal was pale and skinny with soft thinning hair that never quite seemed to sit flat. His eyes were always a little bugged out, too, like he'd just heard the strangest thing and he wasn't sure he appreciated it. He'd been at Bedford Public School since forever. He'd taught Peter's father. The rumour was he'd founded the school single-handedly sometime in the 1800s.

"Peter," he began. "Your mother here—" Ellen shifted and leaned forward in her seat but didn't speak. "That is, your mother has some news to tell you."

"Peter …" Ellen faltered. "Peter, your father. I'm so sorry, Peter dear. Your father has died."

Peter looked at her in shock. It seemed impossible. Unreal. How could she tell him this? How could she sit across from him in his school principal's office, of all places, and tell him this?

"What …"

"It was his heart, Peter," Ellen said. "His heart. It just gave up."

Suddenly, Ellen started to cry. Not a torrent, more a slow leak. Watching the tears trickle from her eyes, Peter caught himself trying to remember the last time she had cried in public. *This really must be happening,* he thought. *She'd give anything not to cry.*

"It just stopped."

Peter watched her closely. His brain told him she was telling the truth, but he felt nothing. The moment dragged on and on and on. Nobody spoke. Peter began to worry about feeling nothing. Who could feel nothing at news like this? He must be a monster to feel nothing when his mother had just told him this.

Suddenly the room seemed like a vacuum. There was

no air. He couldn't breathe. He tried to ask a question —
any question — to try to make it real, but he couldn't get a
noise out. He stared at his mother like she was a stranger.
Mr. Patterson said something. Peter missed it all.

Ellen sat rigid, methodically shredding tissues into a
little snowdrift on her lap, white on white. Breathing wasn't
getting any easier. Peter wondered if death could be conta-
gious and another part of him wondered how he would tell
Mary-Beth, how he would tell anyone. Stupidly, he caught
himself wondering how to tell his dad.

"Your mom found him, Peter," Mr. Patterson said. "Just
like he was asleep across his desk."

Ellen nodded. "I'm so sorry, Peter. This is so out of the
blue. So terrible."

"But he'd already passed," Mr. Patterson concluded.

Passed? Peter's mind got caught up in thinking about
Jack's long-ago principal finally passing him to the next
grade. *Not that kind of passed*, Peter scolded himself. *Pay
attention.* His chest ached. He briefly forgot why they were
there in the office all together, then he remembered and
felt an urge to scream and throw things. His whole class
would know why he'd been called to the office. The news
would get out. Was his father really dead? Was that even
possible? He wanted to drop through the floor and disappear. He didn't know what he wanted.

His stomach felt like someone had stuck a knife in it.
He leaned over and struggled not to puke.

When Jack Weir's funeral took place three days later, the
neighbourhood still littered with empty bottle rockets and
punky jack-o'-lanterns, there was no Nirvana, no party.
Instead, an endless line of men in dark suits gripped Peter's
hand, one after another, an unravelling daisy chain of firm
handshakes and wafts of cologne and shoe polish. It was all
going too fast. None of it seemed real, not the funeral, not
the crowds. Their voices were soft in the church, but later,
back at the house, loud, and Peter didn't like that: it seemed
like disrespect, like his dad was asleep and they should keep
it down.

They all seemed to know what to do and what to say.
Peter kept saying "Thank you" — for what, he wasn't sure.
The more he stood there, uncomfortable in the suit he'd only
worn once before to a cousin's wedding, the angrier he felt.

A man Peter barely recognized, another lawyer maybe,
came up and told Peter how proud he should be of his dad.
For what? Dying? Peter seethed. "He was an example to us
all, a paragon of fidelity and industry." Ellen crossed over to
them from the kitchen, where some of the neighbourhood

women had gathered. She rubbed Peter's arm and asked him if he'd see to the guests a bit for her, offer them drinks. Peter knew what she was saying: Be a grown-up. Act appropriately. Don't yell. Save the tears for later.

"Yeah, Mom. Of course." Peter excused himself and threaded his way through this roomful of strangers standing around on Ellen's carpet (*with their shoes on!*). He'd never felt so alone in his life, surrounded by all these well-meaning people who couldn't understand a single thing that was going through his mind. Mary-Beth caught his eye and wiggled her eyebrows. *Outside?* Peter was tempted but he knew that Mary-Beth would want to talk and Peter was sick of talking. He had nothing left to say and even being quiet together felt too nice for the worst day of his life. He shook his head. Mary-Beth looked hurt. Across the room, Ellen started toward him but got cut off by a semicircle of golfers, the very ladies she'd been with before she came home to ... It was all too much. Nobody understood. Not his mom. Not his best friend. Nobody. Peter went upstairs to hide. They'd all have to leave sometime.

CHAPTER TWO

There was nothing special about the day Peter ran away, either. Anyone who says you can tell what's coming next is lying: stuff just happens, and there's no way to prepare for it. Destiny is the biggest fairy tale there is. Of course, others would say that proves something else. You're on your own. Always be prepared.

The dawn was cold and clear, though. That much was true.

"Peter! It's 8:10! I'm not having you miss that bus. Get yourself down here!"

Peter sighed. His mother was on the warpath. Again. In the week since his dad died, she'd been like herself, only more so. It mattered to her that he get up and make it in to school. Even the very next day. He could do that much for her, he guessed. With a sigh, he squinted up out of his old beat-up *Phantom Menace* duvet, across his little attic bedroom, and through the slit of window between the drawn curtains. Cold and clear. And hard. Today would be a hard day. Another hard day. Peter wasn't sure he was up to it. He'd barely slept. Even when he did, it was more like dozing. It didn't feel like it counted. He was getting more and more worn out. And another thing: no dreams. He hadn't had one dream since the day he'd come home from Mr. Patterson's office to the empty, silent house.

The days passed. There was no question of letting go, giving in, giving up. Only errands and paperwork and projects, the chief one being Peter himself.

Peter struggled into a sitting position. Some car ad on the radio. Ads were even worse than music. Ads meant 8:15. He should get up. He should totally get up. He wouldn't put it past his mother to come up for him. *Now* she made breakfast for him. Every morning, a hot breakfast that neither one of them had the appetite to eat. The first morning, that terrible first morning after, he'd set his chair as far away from his father's spot as he could. There was a smell, the smell of frying bacon. His mother had brought him a plate piled with food, but she moved in slo-mo, like a John Woo movie.

The plate lowered, second by second, closer and closer.

"Um, I can't eat this. I'm sorry."

Silence.

More silence.

"Yes, Peter. Yes you can." Her voice was compressed, like when the signal on the cellphone goes all weak, a faint copy of her original voice seeping through. Those normal days, which had seemed like such a struggle at the time, were a million miles away now. Farther than the farthest satellite. He missed them with an ache that was like holding your breath from one end of the pool to the other.

He pushed back his plate, then caught his mother's eye. Blank. Peter flashed on a conversation they'd had during a break in some sappy movie-of-the-week a while back, the three of them squished onto the sofa in the living room. His dad got up to answer the phone (his clients never seemed to understand there was a work number and a home number, a confusion Ellen often pointed out wouldn't exist if Jack didn't hand out both numbers to the ninety percent of his clients he considered "friends") and Peter and his mom had one of those talks that are only half-serious because you know the show is going to come back on any second and you're just talking to drown out the commercial. (He'd begged for TiVo. Begged.)

"Mom, what would you do if Dad and I were in comas?"

"You mean like in this silly movie?"

"Yeah. If there was no way of knowing whether we'd ever wake up. What would you do?"

"What a question, Peter! I don't know. But I know one thing I would not do. I would *not* sit in the hospital cafeteria and pour out my soul to every sorry stranger who wheels through on their way outside for a cigarette." Ellen had this way of drawing out that "s" sound in cigarette, like a rattle-snake. It was one of Peter's favourite Ellenisms to imitate. *Sssssssssssigarette*. She had this way of wrinkling up her nose at the same time and baring her teeth. It was so perfect.

Then the show had come back on and Jack had run back in and that was that.

At that first breakfast without Jack, Peter had wondered if his mother remembered the coma talk. She gave him the look again. This was not a question he could ask. He lowered his fork to the plate, opened his mouth, and ate.

"Peter!" came the call again.

"I heard you, Mom!" Music. Ads. Music.

So tired. He'd raced for the bus the day before and lost, slipping and skidding on the ice-slick streets. He'd lost his footing. His get-up-and-go just got up and went.

Another Ellenism. Peter threw aside the duvet, struggled to his feet, and grabbed whatever had oozed to the top of the clothes mound during the night. Dressing by Darwin. He dragged himself thump thump thump down the stairs and into the kitchen, choked down scrambled eggs and toast, folded himself into a parka and basically fell out the door.

School was another problem. School took energy too. The kids were talking. Not ragging exactly, but not leaving him alone either. Circling, probing. Needling. To Peter, the buzz was like the drill at the dentist's. Kids asking him how he was. Kids not asking how he was, turning around when they saw him and going a different way. Whispering as he passed by. Giving these tight little smiles that were supposed to say something profound about something. None of it hurt, but the noise was getting on his nerves. And his nerves were already sore. He just wanted the noise and the pressure to stop, at home and at school.

Which is how the fight started.

He heard Alex Carlton say it to Dennis Chan as he brushed past on his way to the library for a spare. At least the library was quiet — as in, deserted.

Peter stopped in the hall, turned slowly, and squinted at the two boys.

"What did you say?"

"What? Nothing, man. I didn't say nothing."

But Peter couldn't let it go. Besides, he'd heard it. "Yes you did, Alex. Say it again."

"I said … I didn't say nothin'. Forget it, man."

But Alex's eyes told a different story. Alex's eyes said *Dare me.*

Peter took a step closer, and the drifts of kids shifted. It was like in the car ads, when they show the wind tunnels. You see the car and you see the air around the car, and if you look at it right, if you pay attention, it's the air that holds the shape of the car, not the other way around. Invisible but solid, close as breath, it's a wind to fall into, a wind that could hold you up, show you where you stop and the rest of the world begins, for when you forget.

Alex looked at Dennis, at the other kids around him, then shrugged.

"All I said was, what are you doing here anyway, is all. I mean, if my dad …" Alex trailed off. His eyes swung left and right.

"Freak," Dennis coughed into his hand.

Peter didn't care what Alex thought of him or his dad. He didn't care about Dennis. He didn't care about any of the kids staring from their lockers at the boys toe to toe in an emptying slice of hall. He didn't even care that the buzzer for second class would ring in a minute, maybe two. He just wanted it all to stop. All the whispering, all the

avoiding eye contact. The gossip. The ache. Even the breakfasts. The groggy mornings when he opened his eyes but
felt like he was still asleep. Just to stop. So he hit big, fat,
slow Alex Carlton right between the eyes.

"Fight! Fight!"

The kids, girls and boys alike, sent the chant along the
halls, their suburban faces aglow with the promise of
excitement and violence. Banana time in the monkey cage.
Whoop-de-doo.

Even as Peter was plugging away at Alex — who was
surprisingly strong and made up for his slowness with some
not insignificant blows to the gut — he could hear the chatter
around him. He'd forgotten about that. Wind tunnels were
noisy, too.

"What is his problem, anyway?"

"They are such losers."

"Totally! Did you notice? Peter's been wearing those
same clothes, like, all week!"

"He is so immature. I mean, really."

This last comment from a girl Peter had made out with
at a party last summer, the two swaying out of time to the
Stone Temple Pilots, chrysalises by the millions bursting
into butterflies in his stomach. Yeah, well, too bad.

And Mary-Beth at the other end of the corridor, shut
out from the crowd circling him and Alex. Mary-Beth who

looked neither happy nor unhappy. Who just shrugged one shoulder to hike up a bag of books as she crunched into an apple as red as a stoplight from this distance. But there was no stopping for Peter. And as the bell sounded, Mary-Beth turned and disappeared, her face unreadable.

And more punches, finally followed by "Peter. Alex. I want to see you both in my office. Right now."

Both kids ended up with an afternoon detention, which was getting off lightly, but Peter never served his. At two o'clock, he was called into the school office. An immaculate Ellen was there to take him across town to meet the lawyer about his father's estate. From the moment Peter fastened his seat belt, Ellen never looked his way. Hands firmly at ten and two, she was the model of caution, practically an ad for Young Drivers, performing every task with almost robotic precision. Peter watched her for a moment, then turned toward his window and let his eyes unfocus and his brain slide.

Finally, side by side in the lawyer's underground parking lot, the stilled engine ticking softly, Ellen reached across and tried to smooth her son's spastic curls.

"Peter …"

"Mom. It's okay. Let's just go inside."

Ellen undid her seatbelt, let it roll up into its dispenser, then twisted over to face him. "No, Peter. I know how hard things are for you right now, how sad. What I mean is, I've been … distracted these last few days. I know that. I know what you're going through. You don't think I do, but I do. You know, hard as it is to believe, I was fourteen once —"

"I'm almost fifteen."

"I was almost fifteen once. I even remember what it was like. Maybe after all this is over and done with, after the will and all the affairs are wrapped up —"

"Mom. I'm fine. We're going to be late. You hate being late."

Was he sad? It wasn't a word he would have chosen. *Pissed off*, sure. *Cheated*, definitely. *Tired*. He felt the way he had after Alex landed that first fist, like breathing was more trouble than it was worth, like something fine had been ripped out of his chest and thrown away. He felt like standing up straight might snap his spine. Peter understood why the intrepid trapper, mauled by the polar bear, just wanted to lie down in the snow, just for a minute, just for a rest.

Hugh O'Connell had been a classmate of Jack Weir's. His handshake had come to the funeral. Probably his after-shave, too, which Peter could smell from the door now.

Weak afternoon sun slanted through the Venetian blinds. Bookcases filled with wide binders and hardcover books that looked like encyclopedias rose on all sides to a ceiling of speckled acoustic tiles. The air smelled of dust and, faintly, hot oil and sugar from the doughnut place downstairs.

"Peter. Ellen," Mr. O'Connell began, running his hand over his mouth and down his chin. "Again, let me say how sorry I am for your loss." He indicated two chairs as he moved around the desk to his own seat in front of the windows.

"If there's any silver lining — if I may put it that way," he paused to smile apologetically at each of them, "it's that this will be very straightforward. Jack had his affairs in order, of course, so there are no surprises there. No surprises at all. The man was impeccable. A real professional." His expression demonstrated just how silver that lining was. He paused again, looked back and forth between Peter and his mother for something he clearly expected to find but didn't, then hurried on.

"Nevertheless, the execution of an estate requires some signatures. As we discussed, Ellen. And there's Peter's trust fund to see to. It will be your father's legacy, Peter, to help you find your way in life, which I'm sure you'll come to appreciate as you grow older."

Peter tried to pay attention, but the sun through the

blinds was warm and Mr. O'Connell had turned his attention back to the papers stacked on his desk, reading aloud first from one, then another. Peter struggled to keep his eyes open.

Mr. O'Connell was holding out a plain letter-size envelope. Its front was blank white.

"Peter. There's one more thing. Your father never knew, of course, how tragically short his life would be." He turned to Ellen briefly and paused, then continued. "But he put this aside, for you. Just in case. Now, it's a lot of money just to hand over — a thousand dollars. He called it 'a little seed' from your fund, something to give you some choices, for after he, well, for after he passed on."

"Oh, Hugh," Ellen jumped in. "Jack never mentioned this to me. Is it really such a good idea? Just handing over cash like this?" She smiled weakly at Peter, but continued to address the lawyer. "I'll hold on to it until we can get to a bank. Heaven knows Peter is forgetful. And his room! Put something in there and you might as well say goodbye to it forever." She chuckled to herself, like this was somehow funny, and reached across to pat Peter's knee. She was on the edge of her chair, and tugging down on her skirt as she reached over for the envelope.

"I'm sorry, Ellen. This is a bit awkward, but Jack left specific instructions. For nobody but Peter. For his own use.

I tried to change his mind, especially in cash like this. But Jack wouldn't budge. He always had a dramatic side to him, even in school. As far as Jack's wishes go, what the boy does with this envelope is up to him and him alone."

Peter didn't like "the boy." That snapped him out of his stupor.

"I'll take it, Mr. O'Connell." His hand was out before he was even aware of it. He felt his mother's eyes on him but continued, slowly and carefully: "It's from Dad. I'll keep it safe."

When they got home there was a message from Mr. Patterson. Could Ellen make it back into school before five? Peter's mother shot him a look, phone cradled between chin and shoulder, sighed, and looked at her watch. She speed-dialed the school and told the secretary she could be there in ten minutes, sparing Peter a glare as she did so. He just shrugged. Hadn't he mentioned the fight? She hung up, crossed to the fridge and poured Peter a glass of milk, talking the whole time, half to Peter, half to herself.

"We'll have lasagna and salad for dinner. I'll take the lasagna out of the freezer. When the oven's up to temperature, put it in and set the timer for an hour. Will I be back by then?

Yes, I should be back by then. And don't spend all your time in front of the TV. You've got homework to do. School can't stop just because …"

She paused and her mouth tightened. She'd been jarred into realizing where she was, what she was saying in that moment. Peter watched with interest. For once, his mind was completely clear. He had no idea what she would do next. "Think twice, speak once" — another Ellenism. But that was from his old life, from before. After a few moments, she exhaled, turned and left the room.

As she scooped up her car keys, she called back: "What I'm trying to say, Peter, is that you still have responsibilities. To your teachers and yourself."

Peter listened to the quiet that settled after her departure, to the thrum of the fridge, the muted yells of kids playing hide-and-seek outside. *Ready or not, here I come!*

He wandered through the house, fiddling, remembering. Every corner held memories. Messy Sunday brunches. French toast or poached eggs. Tea with milk and double sugar for three. The weekend paper splayed across the table, Peter reading everyone their horoscopes. Or just companionable silences that felt more comfortable than the new heavy stillness. He missed his dad, of course, but he missed his mom too, he realized, his mom who could shrug her shoulders. "I put my trust in the gods," she used to say.

Peter had a feeling he wouldn't be hearing that much anymore.

Images continued to crowd in. Pottering in the basement. Mowing the lawn for allowance money, his dad pretending not to watch from the upstairs window in case Peter mulched the power cord. Trips to the hardware store for light bulbs and washers. Nothing big. Just stuff. Guy stuff he would never share again. The endless projects that the two of them embarked on with such enthusiasm, even though they almost never got to the end: half-finished models, aborted science-fair projects, a lava lamp waiting for a last few components to get groovy. The lecture he got from his dad the day he finally received his own penknife, which he'd been begging for basically every day since he'd learned the word. His dad displaying the ancient shadow of a scar across his thumb where he cut himself, deep, carving pine cones when he was a kid himself. "Do as I say, Peter. Not as I do." Duh! Once it was November, like now, Jack usually liked to put some thought into Christmas themes. Hanging Christmas lights was one of Peter's earliest memories. Just one image, really, of his own red-mittened hand clutching a loop of lights and twisting them around the banister at the front of the house. He must have been maybe four. Sometimes, he thought he could recall feeling pukey as he did it, that he was up on the big wooden ladder with the lights, the one that always gave that spongy feeling when you stood on it, even if someone was at the bottom to hold it steady.

Peter started back to the kitchen to check on the oven, but the effort seemed beyond him. Tears stung his eyes, and he felt he was about to lose it. He thought about calling Mary-Beth. But Peter couldn't stand the thought of having to talk to Mrs. Kennedy. It was awkward with Mary-Beth now, too. Awkward to think of anything to say, and if he didn't say anything at all, that didn't feel right either. Mary-Beth kept acting like she had to think of just the right question to ask. He should call. He would call. Later.

Peter threw himself onto the sofa — homework, schmomework — and snagged the remote. And felt the extra heft in his back pocket.

Peter broke the seal and flipped through the bills. A thousand bucks. It was unreal, all that money in one place. He would never admit it, but his mother was right. He would lose it if he didn't find somewhere safe. He was going to have to open a bank account and stop spending every penny the second it fell into his hands. (*Is that why you left me this, Dad? Is this some kind of test?*) In the meantime, his room was no place for valuables.

Peter's hand reached around the corner and automatically hit the switch as he entered his father's study. He hadn't been in the room since before Jack died and the sight of it stopped him cold. He stared at the desk for a few minutes. The very desk where his dad used to help him with science homework, which would've been great — Peter had no hard and fast definitions when it came to teamwork — except that "help" in this scenario was a synonym for "supply," Jack being maybe better at law than at science. Peter was getting a solid C+ in science, and that was actually down from the term before, when he had to make it all up on his own. "Dad, I don't think Wikipedia is exactly what Mrs. Musio had in mind when she said we need to research the diffraction of light waves."

But it was just a desk. It didn't *mean* anything at all. Or did it? Was there something to be learned from it, something about death or his father's last thoughts? Had he known? What had he felt in that instant between life and death? Fear? Peace? Had he bargained, made promises in order to get a little more time? Peter tried to remember how his dad had looked that last morning, at the table with a cup of coffee before "the big commute," his joke about the trip down the hall. He tried to imagine those final seconds.

It was just a desk.

Peter didn't mean to snoop. He just wanted to find a safe stash for the money, somewhere out of harm's way — and Ellen's. His mother would eventually go through all the drawers, but not for a few days. Not even Ellen. From the kitchen he heard the oven ping. *Houston, prepare for lasagna.*

We learn through osmosis. Peter had read that. We add new facts to those we already have, like slotting bricks into an ever-growing wall. Sometimes we learn without meaning to, the gaps waiting, the bricks suddenly there. It's not even always on a conscious level. Maybe that's why Peter headed so naturally around the desk, opened the bottom drawer, and squatted in front of the press of files straining to accordion up and out. He yanked the drawer open to its full extension and slid out the last manila folder.

He'd hide the money at the back, shut it away until he could think clearly. His dad must have had some reason for giving him this money. There must be a message in among all those fifties. One good night's sleep and maybe he could decipher it. Peter paused over the open folder, about to drop the wad of money in, and noticed an envelope already inside, a skinny twin to the one in his hand.

At the sight of his father's scrawl on the outside of it, Peter felt something. Call it precognition or instinct. Or maybe there is such a thing as fate. Was it an accident, this discovery?

Or was it meant to be? Somehow, just from the surface of that envelope, from the quality of the writing or the pressure of the ink, he knew that whatever was inside was about to change his life forever.

Peter looked closer to read the word on the envelope: *Adoption.*

CHAPTER THREE

Peter was a mess. Literally. He had a quarter of an apple turnover in one hand and he was covered in crumbs. He was trying to make the remains of his lunch last, so he only let himself take a bite every four minutes. Checking his watch, there were still one hundred seconds until he was allowed to finish the last piece. In the meantime, he licked his fingers and tried to dab up crumbs. Ninety seconds.

Outside the bus window, dirt fields unrolled, remarkable only for how completely unremarkable they were. It was just past noon, Peter was tired and sore, and the bus was somewhere on the prairies, heading west. Even with the tinted windows, the harsh light hurt his eyes.

He hadn't had a shower in two days and he figured he probably didn't smell too good. His hair was, well, forget about it, and he'd been napping in his clothes, half an hour at a stretch, ever since he had run out of the house and wound up at the bus station. It had almost felt like a normal school morning: Peter running, always running, his backpack still full of homework over one shoulder. But now with two envelopes in his pockets, one containing money, one containing ... No, he wouldn't think about that. He'd already spent two days not thinking about that. Thirty seconds.

The batteries for his Discman died just then, so there was nothing to do but watch the sticks speed by.

He sighed and checked his watch again, remembering his idea about bomb timers and countdowns. A million years ago.

3 ... 2 ... 1 ... Yes! Turnover time!

"In a hurry, young man?"

Peter started and pulled out his earphones. The old woman in the seat next to him had got on in some little nowhere town, but this was the first time she'd spoken.

He must have looked blank as he stuffed the last of the precious junk-foody goodness into his mouth, because she smiled. "You keep on looking at your watch like that and you're going to wear it out. Have a bus to catch?"

"Umm, ha," he managed around the pastry. "No. No hurry.

I'm not getting off till the coast. I just … keep forgetting what time it is."

He knew that sounded lame, but it was better than explaining the Peter Weir Snack System.

"It's hard to wait, isn't it?" She smiled again, and Peter could tell he was in for it. Just his luck. What was it about him that made every old lady feel like she was his honorary grandmother? The bus could be full of kids, and twenty times out of twenty, it would be Peter they all zeroed in on. Maybe this one had food …

"When I was a girl, of course, nobody flew anywhere. We took trains then, and they didn't even travel as quickly as this bus does now." She leaned over and patted his arm. "But then, we had a different notion of time in those days, I suppose. We didn't expect to arrive anywhere very quickly, so we didn't have the same need always to be in such a hurry."

She beamed at Peter, and he couldn't tell if he was supposed to reply, so he gave something that was part nod, part stretch and part resettling in his seat. Couldn't she tell he was in no mood to chat? Didn't he look like a desperate dropout on the run? Didn't she have any instincts for self-preservation? He could be anyone. Maybe life on the prairies was more trusting than back in the city. Peter caught himself feeling he should explain Stranger Danger to this farm-town granny. Who was, he realized, talking again.

Peter closed his eyes and imagined Mary-Beth pulling some little snack out of her backpack. Her bangs would swing in front of her eyes as she rummaged, and she'd tuck them behind one ear. There'd be no rush. Mary-Beth had never rushed anywhere in her life, as far as Peter knew. He tried to remember even one instance of her rushing, but drew a blank. He could call, from the next truck stop maybe, and ask. He owed her a call. *Mary-Beth, when was the last time you were late for something?* But just the thought was enough to exhaust him. Mary-Beth and her perfect, orderly life. Her perfect, no-hidden-secrets family. There was something that stood between them now. It didn't feel like they were two against the world, the way they had been before Peter's life folded into itself like an origami version of hell.

As though she'd read his mind, the elderly lady asked him, "Visiting family?"

"Excuse me?"

"Are you travelling to visit family, dear?"

"Oh! Umm … yeah. I'm staying with my aunt and uncle for a couple of weeks. My aunt and uncle on my dad's side. I'm on, um, independent study!"

There was nothing true about this statement, but it was what he'd told the ticket agent back home and it sounded believable. (Can't a nearly-fifteen-year-old go anywhere without questions these days?) Peter didn't have any uncles or aunts, and since he'd only bought a one-way ticket, peeling off eight of the fifties from the "little seed" he had stuffed in his jeans pockets, he had no idea how long he'd be travelling. More than a couple of weeks, though, that was for sure. As far as he was concerned, he would be happy if he never went back to that quiet house and the careful breakfasts and the hidden secrets and his mother's insistence that the best way to get on with life was just to get on with it. What kind of philosophy was that? Peter found himself wondering guiltily what it would be like if it had been Jack who'd survived, Ellen who'd died. Would it have made things easier? Would he be on this bus, with a hole where his old normal life, his former so-called happy childhood used to be? What if it had been Jack who'd come home to … But there was no changing things now, not his father's death, not his adoption. None of it. Peter thought of how Ellen would cope. *The best way to get on with life is just to get on with it.*

Yeah? Live through this, Mom.

Peter shook his head to clear his thoughts and glanced out the bus window at the passing landscape. It was a world without people, without anything he could call hope. The words came back, the same words that had beat a constant refrain since the station. *Adopted! And they never even told me! It's not right!* Every mark on that paper was seared into his memory. A government form. His parents' names — could he still call them parents? A stamp from the director of child services.

He'd never seen it coming. Not even close. It was like something out of a movie-of-the-week. Or a nightmare. But which version of his life was the nightmare, and which was real? Was his former life with its lies the nightmare and had he finally woken up? Or was he in the middle of a nightmare now? Maybe he'd wake up in his old attic room with two parents — two real parents — downstairs waiting for the morning tornado to pass through on its way to school?

Peter thought back to all the times his mother had laughed at him and his dad together, puzzling over some project in the basement. Now that Peter thought about it, maybe Jack's "help" with the science homework explained a lot about why their special undertakings never really panned out. Peter had fond memories of a birdhouse the two of them had made, back when Jack was going through his environmental phase. Jack was always going on about how the neighbourhood cats were a menace to birds, so Peter had found a birdhouse plan on a website. The birdhouse was supposed to provide shelter for small birds during their flight south in winter. But physics definitely wasn't their strong suit — or maybe it was, maybe they'd discovered some new dimension where small birds, exhausted from the first leg of their annual trip, could phase-shift their bodies out of the too-small birdhouse with its unfinished perch, its constricting doorway that nearly beheaded a family of finches. Ellen wasn't so sure. Surveying the scraps and the mess, she'd just shaken her head: "You two! You're like two peas in a pod." Peter hadn't liked her saying it then. He knew she thought his dad was disorganized, a slob even. That he couldn't be bothered reading the fine print ("Fine print is for lawyers!" he liked to scoff). He'd never thought he was anything like his parents. On the one hand, Ellen and her golf and her lunches and her causes. Ellen and her hair always in place and her knack for knowing the right place to buy flowers and the right colour shoes. And on the other hand, Jack and his study bulging with the paperwork of other people's lives. His lame jokes. His puppy-dog friendliness. He couldn't walk to the corner store without making six new best friends.

As he looked back now, though, Peter missed the comfortable feeling he'd never bothered to notice at the time. He remembered his confidence about the dark, that he could walk the maze of rooms with his eyes shut. Wrong. All that time the envelope lay buried in the desk in his father's study, a dark heart pumping out the family's secret blood. He was nothing like Ellen, nothing like Jack even. Peas in a pod? Wrong.

"... with all the rain."

Peter caught his breath. He'd tuned out again.

"Yeah, definitely. Umm ... would you excuse me, please?" He pointed across her seat to the corridor and the lady tottered to her feet to let him past.

Peter made his way to the rear, struggling to keep his balance as the bus jolted its way across the grasslands. He tried not to mind how many of the people he passed were travelling *with* someone, how freakish he felt thousands of miles from home, father dead, no plan in mind except just to keep on moving. There was nobody he'd be sharing his alien zoo cage with today.

At the back, three kids sprawled along the rear seats. They looked about his age, but tough, all three of them, especially the one with his legs blocking the doorway to the bathroom.

Peter looked at the ground, at the boy's feet, at the door. This could be a problem.

"'Scuse me."

"Oh," the tall boy spoke with exaggerated politeness. "I beg your pardon. Did you say 'Excuse me'?" He turned to his friends and snickered. Peter noticed a rip in the neck-band of his Limp Bizkit tour shirt, tattoo blue underneath.

"I just need to get past. Move your legs?"

"No. I can't move my legs. They're sleeping. Step over."

The kid held one finger to his lips to shush them all, then rolled his eyes to his friends like he was the most hilarious thing since Jim Carrey.

More like the ugliest.

Peter lifted one foot over the boy's legs, pretty sure about what was going to happen next. Sometimes there's an inevitability. It was like with Alex in the hall at school. Or like boarding the bus: you pay your money in one place and there's nothing to do then but wait until you're in some other city a continent away and what's left of your family has no idea, absolutely no idea, where you are, or even who you are. And you have no idea yourself.

The meathead swung his leg up and sideways to knock Peter off-balance. Without even consciously deciding, Peter allowed the momentum to spin him a quarter-circle and then he let himself fall, landing on the boy's other leg, still stretched out in the corridor. He could feel the bones inside bend as they took his weight. It wasn't a natural position. The boy screamed.

Peter was already off the leg, in a crouch in front of all three of them, fists balled, his back to the bathroom door. His mind was empty. There was no sound in the wind tunnel this time, except the long pained echo of that yell. The worries of the last week faded away, and weirdly, given how completely homicidal all three kids looked, Peter felt peace.

Then a staticky squawk came from overhead and the driver called over the PA: "Keep it down at the back there, fellas. Some folks're tryin' to sleep."

"Tough guy, eh?" the first kid growled at Peter. He was bending and unbending his leg, breathing through his mouth. "We'll see about that."

"I just wanted the can," Peter replied, but he spun around and headed back to his seat, where he stuck his 'phones back in his ears and listened furiously to the silence.

When Peter finally got to the coast, he wasn't feeling so hot. The one guy he maybe could have handled, after his like, three days as a *Matrix*-style kung fu killer orphan, but not all three of them.

They were skinny, sure, but muscled and tall, and city boy Peter never had much of a chance. Probably he should have just stayed on the bus when it pulled in for a pit stop and gas-up. But the call of a burger and a milkshake was so strong that Peter hadn't given too much thought to the Three Stooges as he clambered off the bus and headed for the diner across the parking lot. Mistake. He found himself grabbed, lifted, and carried around back — in full view of every single person he'd been sharing that coach with.

And it hadn't been long before he had a blackening eye, a cut along the brow that wouldn't stop bleeding and a finger that felt like maybe it was busted. Not only that, but they'd taken his wallet, all but the four fifties he had stashed in his backpack, and the Discman out of his pocket, and run off. Easy come. Hard go.

"Hrrrrgh," Peter'd said to a slick of oil and water an inch from his nose, which translated into something like "Welcome to my glamorous life." He'd just been considering a little nap there on the asphalt, which was actually quite comfy if you closed your eyes against the sun — slow slosh of blood, wolves circling — when he'd heard the coach toot its move-it-or-lose-it call. He should get up. He should totally get up. He told himself to stand. He was very firm about it, but it was like his body had decided no more orders from the brain. *Maybe they damaged something*, he thought to himself. *Something important. Some kind of brain thing and I'm going to end up in a wheelchair on Timmy's Telethon. Great.* Time stretched out like the surface of a soap bubble, shiny and swirling. Like oil on water in a grimy parking lot halfway from nowhere to nowhere.

Peter's mind felt truly empty, peaceful even. The most peace he'd felt since his dad died. It was a relief. All the doubts and insecurities were still there, but muted. Like he could see all his troubles, but they were behind a smudgy pane of glass. His worries were on the other side of a window now, and he couldn't open that window if he wanted. For once, Peter was completely out of control. It was a feeling he liked.

The moment stretched on.

The bus honked again, shattering his fuzzy peace. Timeout was over. Peter levered himself painfully off the ground and swayed across the asphalt, up the steps into the bus and back into his seat. His neighbour, who had ignored him since the altercation outside the bus bathroom, only tsked when she saw the blood. A nice little grandma bag of butter tarts wasn't seeming so likely after all.

Peter forced his eyes open and willed away the tears. He twisted his head as far back around his shoulder as he could manage. Something popped deep in his neck.

Nothing stirred across the cracked surface of the truck stop's apron: the three hoodlums were long gone. As the coach pulled back out onto the highway, though, the sun glinted off something against the dull lake of black asphalt. Peter quickly jammed his hands into his pockets. It was his penknife, a present from his dad. It had fallen out during the fight, and the punks had rammed it into the ground up to the hilt. It dwindled into the distance and was gone.

CHAPTER FOUR

This city wasn't what he'd expected. Cold and clear back home was cold and wet here. And grey. Peter and his family had travelled, but they'd always headed for sun, somewhere hot and exotic and cheap. *Not cheap. Reasonable, Peter dear.* One year they'd visited a string of museums and galleries for his mom, which was more like a school trip than a vacation, but still better than this. Was this what he'd spent all this time leaving home for?

The bus station was in a bad part of town, same as back home. Not somewhere Ellen had encouraged Peter to hang out. Now he felt like a Boy Scout heading into a Wild West saloon. Peter tried to walk tall, like there was a new hombre in town and the sidewalk was his. *Walk like a brick wall*, the cops who came to school every year said. But with only his half-empty backpack and his bulging parka for protection, he felt about as tough as the Stay Puft Marshmallow Man from *Ghostbusters*. He slouched and his mouth went dry. The evening streets were mostly deserted. What day was it, anyway? Monday the eleventh. *Remembrance Day*, Peter realized, remembering red poppies blazing out from shabby lapels. *Remembrance Day, and I forgot. Okay, not funny.*

He felt like prey.

A plan would have been good, he told himself. *What were you doing for three days on the bus, anyway? Oh yeah, doling out the junk food and getting beat up.* That final day, after the fight, was a new definition of painful. Scraped, robbed and wounded in his body and his pride. Peter couldn't make eye contact with anyone. It was a relief just to get off the bus and be able to start over. And it could be worse. He still had the four fifties. He'd start with a night somewhere cheap. And in the morning? That was a decision for the morning.

He had a terrible night in the hostel that night, unaccustomed noises and shufflings through the dark hours. That part was like summer camp, but there was the worry about what he would do next. It was one thing to run away from home, dump school, blow his money, cross the country. But eventually he had to quit running and make some decisions. Didn't he? All night he tossed and turned, replaying conversations. He thought about Mary-Beth a lot, about all the times they'd promised to look out for each other, to be a team. About how they agreed once back in sixth grade that they would both become doctors and move to Africa together to save the babies. (Nice plan, except Peter was failing math.) He thought about how her life now just carried on while his had fallen apart. It wasn't fair. He felt rage toward Mary-Beth, and then guilty to be so mad at her.

He felt guilty about Ellen, too. Guilty enough that when the hostel windows showed that it was daytime (it all felt the same to him), he left the building in search of a phone. That was a plan. Phone. Food. Then … something.

His mother hadn't changed the message on the answering machine, and he shivered when he heard his father's voice. Ghostly. Rattled, Peter gripped the pay phone and felt the seconds slip away, visualized them as apple turnover crumbs dropping into the pay phone, numbers scrolling down on the bomb timer.

Finally, he felt foolish just standing there on the sidewalk, holding the receiver, not saying anything. He took a deep breath and spoke. "Hi, Mom. It's me. Peter." He tried to imagine what she might be doing. He didn't even know what time it was back home. Would she be out searching the neighbourhood? Checking the video arcades? She knew he sometimes hung out at Neon Peon, the place down on Market Street where all the neighbourhood kids went after school. It was weird because there were two arcades across the street from each other — Electric Circus and Neon Peon — but for some unspoken reason, nobody ever went to Electric Circus, which had a nicer building and even occasional sunshine through the front window. (Maybe that's why no one went?) Neon Peon had glamour, too. Gossip had it that Mike Magee, the owner, had been kicked out of Bedford Public School after he crazy-glued all the doors shut and pulled the fire alarm. Panic ensued. He said it was real-life research into crowd behaviour (he was trying to figure out how Super Mario could get through a locked-door maze) but the teachers didn't agree and Mr. Patterson — who was, like, two hundred even then — had expelled him. The story went that as he left, Magee had shouted, "Fine! Who cares if I can't keep coming here? But I'm not going away. I'll figure out some way to keep all the kids out of your dumb school as much as possible." Neon Peon was another thing Jack and Ellen had argued about, although even Jack couldn't really come up with excuses for Mike Magee, who looked like he'd walled himself in a video arcade years ago and hadn't seen fresh air, a shower or a comb since. Actually, that was probably pretty accurate.

Ellen had no doubt been there already and asked around about him. And at the mall. Plus she was probably phoning all his friends. Could the police be involved yet? It felt like a lifetime, but he'd only been gone four days. The goodbye note he'd left beside the lasagna on the counter read, *Can't stay. I'll call.* Oh dammit, he'd left the oven on. Ellen would be mad about that too.

Peter straightened. What if she was just pretending that nothing had happened? That he hadn't run away? That he was at a sleepover or on a school trip or something? She'd told him he should just get back to normal as quickly as possible. "There's no point ending your own life just because your father's has ended." And she was right, in a way. "Your father wouldn't want that, now would he?" Peter felt confused. Was it possible she would try to follow her own advice? Was she right now advancing on the sand trap by the fifteenth hole, the one that always put her over par, acting like her husband and son were snug back home, watching some old Marx Brothers comedy on TV? Like everything was peachy keen? He had to concede it was possible. But surely not likely.

"Mom, um, when you get this message? Don't panic. I know you're probably freaking, but really, I'm fine.

Don't worry about me. I should have waited, tried to explain or something, I know, but … well … we all have things we should have tried to explain, right?"

He looked up into the sky. "Like telling me I'm adopted … How 'bout that, huh?" It was still raining, and it looked like night was falling, although it wasn't even noon yet. A low-slung muscle car growled by, the driver a shadow behind tinted windows. Peter squared his shoulders and leaned into the booth.

"Anyway, don't worry. I'm safe. I'll try to call again in a day or two. I just … wanted you to know I'm okay and … everything and …"

And what?

"And anyway, don't worry. I've got to go now, Mom. Bye."

As he hung up, all the anger that had fuelled Peter across the country evaporated. He suddenly felt alone, so alone he thought he might start bawling. The misery of his father's death swept through the way the rain was soaking his clothes, and Peter shivered again with a mixture of cold and grief and flat-out exhaustion. His old life felt very far away.

"What you need," he said out loud, "is grease. Lots and lots of hot, delicious grease."

There wasn't much debate, and he headed straight to the McDonald's he'd been to the night before, conveniently located in the ground floor of the hostel. The place was packed with groups of people who all seemed to know each other, hyped on sugar water and cheap protein. They were yelling across the room at each other and there was a food fight going on by the bathroom. *This is just like high school,* Peter thought. *Somehow, I figured life would be different somewhere else.* Since he didn't know anyone and felt shy, he hunkered down over his tray and stolidly worked his way through his not-so-happy meal, trying not to let his mind wander to his finances and how many trips to McDonald's he could afford. Something was going to have to change. The noise and easy friendships got on his nerves — how come some people could have things so easy? — so he finished up and bailed.

Peter headed across the street to one of the pathetic little scraps of mud that seemed to pass for parks in this city and took a bench under the shelter of an old, scarred tree.

Okay, he couldn't put it off any longer.

A dig through his pockets came up with five twenties and almost eighteen bucks in change, mostly quarters. Plus a friendship bracelet from Mary-Beth, a pink eraser, a stick of gum (squashed but still wrapped), house keys (but no house to use them on), one AA battery and a handful of paper — receipts and bus transfers and his detention slip. His backpack yielded three textbooks, his planner, a pencil case and a papery apple core. On top of that, he had the clothes he was wearing and his watch. That was it.

Peter spread his paltry belongings out on the wet bench and started to cry. It was something about how pathetic they looked, how they added up to so much less than a life. He remembered Mary-Beth and him on the bus, no idea what was to come, buttermilk pancakes the only protection against the future.

If I die thees day, you make eet I get proper burial, yes?

He could phone her. He wasn't too good on time zones, but he suspected it was the middle of the day back home. She'd be in school. Anyway, what could she do for him all the way across the country, sitting in some marshy park that smelled like piss and garbage? She still had a life, a home, all those balanced breakfasts to look forward to, plus two parents to make sure she ate up every nutritious crumb. *Save your money for something useful*, he told himself. Another tough-guy car rumbled by and made Peter look around. It really was getting darker. He picked at the scab on his finger (okay, maybe not broken after all, but it hurt a lot) and looked helplessly at this … stuff …

arranged in front of him. Was this how his life was meant to be?

"No use just sitting here taking root," he said in perfect Ellen tones.

Peter balled up the paper scraps and hucked them into a nearby garbage bin. He dropped in the keys too and the eraser, the books, the battery, the apple core and the pencil case after taking out the pencils. And, reluctantly, the bracelet. He held on to the gum — it was all the food he had — and the money.

He felt better with just the essentials. He was bone tired, and it wasn't long, despite the rain and the cold, before the burger and fries worked their magic, and Peter, the empty pack clutched to his chest, began to drift off. His head dropped toward the bench, and he fell into the strangest dream ...

Nothingness. Not the empty black of deep space, with dots of light in the distance, but the nothing of a lack of things, a lack of people, a lack of floor or ground or sky or anything. He was inside a silent bubble that seemed to have no walls or sides or edges of any kind. There was white above him, white beneath, white all around. Even the air itself seemed white, a spongy haze. He remembered that feeling after the three kids had whupped his ass outside the bus. It was like that moment, all his troubles and feelings safely walled off. Only now, it wasn't just physical pain and sadness that were cut off. It was everything. He felt like the Cone of Nothing had been dropped on his head and he had no idea where he was or what was around him. It was not a pleasant sensation. In his dream, he tried to push forward, like an icebreaker nosing through a frozen sea. Peter had never had a dream anything like this before. He didn't even feel like he was asleep — although, come to think of it, what did that prove? *This must be what taking drugs is like,* he thought. He'd known kids who'd done drugs at school, cut classes to smoke dope in the parking lot and play hacky sack. Peter didn't feel much like playing hacky sack right this moment.

He opened his mouth and the whiteness that was all around filled him. In his dream mind, he suddenly wondered if he'd died and risen to a heaven of endless clouds, but he could still feel life beating inside him. This was not death, but something else. *Something wonderful or something terrible?* he wondered.

Lifting his hand he felt fear for the first time: his body had flared into the same whiteness. He was invisible. No, it wasn't that he was invisible; there just wasn't any *him* to him anymore. He was nohim nowhere.

Peter took a breath to scream — and woke up. Just like that. He opened his eyes and the colours of the rathole city park flashed back to life. Too bright. The shriek of traffic and wind and the background chug of the city too loud. Flooded with relief, he felt a flutter of something kindle inside. Sure, he had hardly any money, no friends, no father, and the mystery and betrayal of his adoption bundled up in his back pocket. But he was alive and in one piece. Peter checked his watch and was amazed to see hours had passed since he'd left McDonald's. He'd conked out in the middle of a strange city with nobody to watch over him or even know where he was. *Smooth move, Peter.*

"I'm getting inside," he said, shoving himself off the cold bench.

The job came about because of a cute girl he met at the mall when he went in to shelter from the rain. He was sitting on the edge of the fountain, working up the courage to call Ellen again, when this girl came over and took a place beside him. She was some kind of skinhead with these long bangs in front. A Chelsea, he remembered. Real old-school.

"So, making much?"

Her voice was husky but soft. Her accent said she wasn't from the city. More like a farm somewhere, some place where people didn't speak more than was necessary.

"Sorry?"

"Out of the fountain. I was watching you. You were fishing for pennies."

"Oh," Peter answered, embarrassed. "Not really." There was silence. "But hey, it beats working!"

She just stared in reply, which gave Peter time to take in her brown-and-orange uniform, the streak of flour on her cheek, the kerchief she'd pulled off her head and held in one hand. Oops. Wrong thing to say.

Actually, she didn't seem that angry, more just baffled. "At least I make decent money." Like why would this strange shy boy just sit here all afternoon picking coins out of the water, not even making minimum wage.

"See, my life is a little complicated. I'm just trying to … regroup. You know?"

Looking over at her quiet face, her calm brown eyes in their frame of bangs, Peter thought he wasn't making a whole lot of sense. Minimum wage, on the other hand, made a lot of sense. "I just got here," he continued. "I'm not really sure what I'm going to do next."

They shared a moment of silence.

"You think I could maybe get a job at … Hey, where do you work, anyway?"

She clambered to her feet, stretched and then motioned with a jerk of her chin for Peter to follow.

Her name was Anne, and Taco Shacko was as deadly as it sounded. And Frankie Finucci (Fat Frank, behind his back), who was the owner of this particular franchise, was deadlier still.

When Anne and Peter appeared in the food court, he leaned over the counter, right past a couple dithering over the menu, and yelled so loud that people all the way to the far wall turned their heads. "Hey you, get over here!"

"Hey you!" was Fat Frank's name for anyone who'd ever worked for him.

"Hey you!" he yelled again as Anne got closer. "I been looking for you. I need you back now!"

"But Mr. Finucci, I got another ten minutes on my break still."

"I don't need ten minutes. I need now. That other one, the lazy one, finally quit." Frank shook his head, like the idea of someone quitting was just the latest invention from a world that was losing its grip. His eyes strayed over to Peter, tagging awkwardly along beside Anne.

"I need you to get in here now. What about your friend? He ever run a dishwasher?"

Peter's job interview, conducted in the alcove beside

the huge refrigerator that stored all the Taco Shacko perishables, lasted about one minute.

"You start at six dollars an hour. You wash dishes, prep vegetables, clean up, maybe one day you graduate to mixing sauces."

"Mr. Finucci, that's real decent," Peter began. "But I have this … complication at the bank and they haven't moved my chequing account out here yet, 'cause, see, I just moved from—"

Before Peter could get into the finer points of his utterly fictional financial situation, Fat Frank held up a slab of a finger.

"Hey you, what am I, an idiot? Cash is fine. That's five-fifty, though."

Even that was fine, and Peter maybe could have lasted a while, got to know Anne, built up some savings (except six hours at Taco Shacko exactly equalled the cost of the hostel), lived happily ever after, except — and it was enough to put Peter off pseudo-Mexican world-fusion mallsa-salsa food forever — for Fat Frank.

"Hey you!" Peter was doing his best to figure out the dishwasher, which was a long rectangular silver-metal box with a conveyor belt running through it and a metal lever with a black rubber ball on the end rising from one side. The lever pivoted at the bottom where it connected to the washer.

It was supposed to open the gate-like door to let the dishes out, except it was stuck. The more Peter tugged and yanked, the more stuck it got.

"Hey you!" The yell was so loud this time, Anne dropped an order of bacon chilaquiles onto the floor and Peter, out of some panicked reflex, yanked with maximum force on the handle. It snapped right off.

Fat Frank freaked. He started running through the tiny maze that was the food-prep area, trying to slip his huge burrito-enhanced bulk around fifty-gallon drums of mayo and corn oil. Sideswiping Anne, who was bent over trying to clean up the mess, he stepped in the remains of the chilaquiles, slipped and skidded, then managed to put his foot right through a sack of flour.

A puff of dust rose from the floor, and maybe it was the applause from the food court or maybe it was Peter and Anne bursting out laughing, but Frank hauled off and punched the closest thing to him, which happened to be the microwave. There was a crunch, maybe from the door, maybe from Frank's knuckles. And as Peter stared at the mayhem, the cloud of flour, the smears of bacon and sour cream, the new view hole in the microwave, Frank's furious face, he felt a sudden panic. What was he doing here? He'd gone through the last few days of hell for *this*?

"Sorry, Anne," Peter said as he pulled off his greasy apron. "This just isn't my thing."

She looked from Frank to Peter and back to Frank.

"No. Maybe you're right. See you 'round?"

As Peter made his way through the mall toward the street, he could hear a dwindling cry. "Hey you! Hey you!"

He needed to keep moving. The weather might be different, he might be anonymous, but this city was still too much like home, he realized. He was already settling into a routine, after only three days: wake up at the hostel, watch TV till they kicked him out for the morning, head downstairs to McDonald's for breakfast, then bum around the streets, avoiding the endless rain where possible. He'd been staying away from the mall ever since the Taco Shacko incident. All the way at the other end of downtown, he'd found the library, where they had video games for free in the little kids' area. Stupid video games — and he had to keep an eye out for the librarian, who wasn't hot on him being down there with the toddlers — but video games nonetheless, and free. Free was becoming very important. He was down to maybe twenty-five dollars, which wouldn't pay for another night at the hostel, and he didn't get the impression the staff there were big on charity. Friendly, sure, but he'd already seen them kick two people out, an Australian guy and his girlfriend, for being drunk and rowdy.

Anyway, something has to change, Peter thought to himself. He could be doing all this stuff back home, after all. Hanging out at the library, eating at McDonald's, wandering the streets. What was the point? A thousand bucks and a beating for *this*? Peter remembered Ellen and her advice that each day would be easier than the last. Forget that. Peter didn't want easier. He didn't want things to get better or become routine. He wanted chaos, cataclysmic change, dramatic upheavals. He wanted the sky to go black, the seas to boil, blood to rain down from the heavens. He wanted to wake up an entirely different person. Every day. A rage grew inside him.

What is a person, anyway? The home he comes from and the people he calls parents? Or the clothes he wears, the music he listens to, the games he plays? Maybe it was as easy to change one as the other. Life is unstable, and that felt just about right.

The first thing Peter stole was a pair of scissors. He'd gone back to the mall finally. There really wasn't any choice.

He found himself in Wal-Mart, as big as a city block and three levels high. He was walking through, thinking about Anne and wishing he could buy her a little present to say thanks for the job. She'd been nice. But no matter how cheap the stuff was here, he couldn't afford a single thing. Not if he was going to keep eating. Then he found himself in front of a display of home barber supplies. He stood gazing at the various shiny implements, remembering Anne's strange haircut: long bangs and then peach fuzz on the top of her head. His eyes kept returning to the scissors, long and thin, more like something you'd throw than hold. They were cold and smooth and beautifully shiny in his hand, and they slipped into his parka before the thought had even expressed itself. Peter crossed the deserted floor and took the escalator to the basement.

He found a men's bathroom, deserted. Inside, he pulled out the scissors and admired their sleek design. The weird greenish fluorescent lighting gave everything a flat sameness, like the white haze from his spooky dream. Peter shivered at the memory. Fighting panic, he looked down at his body. Still there. Peter stared at himself in the mirror. "Grow up, chicken." Afraid that he might get busted by a security guard wandering in, he thought about chucking the scissors in the trash. Did he even have anything to feel guilty about? Does shoplifting count if you don't leave the store?

Technically, the scissors were still in Wal-Mart, just not on the same floor. But Peter wasn't sure. His father's legal discussions had never covered anything so … useful.

At first it was hard, especially because he had to stop every time he heard a noise. And the murk didn't help, or the old falling-apart mirror that made everything seem to be scabbing off with leprosy or something. But he persevered, and the floor soon sprouted a crop of brown curls.

No more medium, Peter thought to himself. *From now on, short and simple. Pure.*

The face peering out of the flaking silver was older, the stare harder. It was a tougher face, a survivor's face. Good. He'd need that. The door opened and a customer came in with a screaming two-year-old in tow. Peter quickly slipped the scissors into his pocket and left.

Back upstairs, the new Peter wasn't so worried about the finer points of legal philosophy. He grabbed two pairs of black jeans, two black hoodies, two black T-shirts, and strode into the dressing room. One of each returned to the shelves. And one of each walked out the door. Riding the rush of the five-finger-discount spree, Peter had nailed all the labels and security tags to the change room wall with the tapered hair scissors, which slipped into the drywall like an 8-ball in the side pocket.

In another murky little park, he dumped his old jeans

and plaid shirt, and the stupid parka after transferring the contents from one set of pockets to the other. The old clothes didn't seem right. Anyway, clean slates only come in one colour.

With the new crewcut and the back-in-black clothes, Peter found himself getting a lot more attention from kids his own age, and a lot less from grown-ups. Nobody asked him if he needed help or directions now. Nobody was offering to be his grandma. If they gave him a look at all, it was one of fear. That was one consolation.

TWO FOR THE SHOW

CHAPTER FIVE

"Hey."

"Hey."

Peter nodded at the kid taking the seat next to his, then swung his attention back to his own tray. He was trying to make his cup last so he wouldn't get kicked out, at least not until it stopped raining — if it ever did stop raining on this godforsaken island he'd left the last city to come to. It had been a whim, fleeing the city for somewhere smaller, somewhere farther west. Probably a bad idea, he was starting to realize as he nursed a small Coke for half an hour, doodling all over the paper liner that came with the tray. Now he knew how many slurps it takes to suck up the last drops of melted ice from the bottom of a cup. He forced himself to keep his eyes on his work. He was cross-hatching scales on the back of a dragon. The dragon held Ronald McDonald in his jaws and it didn't look good for the clown. Around the dragon's feet, the Fry Guys were weeping and pleading for Ronald's life. Mayor McCheese held the hilt of a broken sword against the armourlike leg of the giant beast. Good luck. It was McClobbering time.

"Whussup?"

The kid was littler than Peter, thirteen, even twelve maybe, dressed in faded cargo pants and an Eminem T-shirt. He had one of those wallet chains dangling from his belt loop. It scraped the rubber tiles of the floor when he sat down. A long lock of bleached hair swung over one blue-green eye. He gave Peter the once-over as he unwrapped a double cheeseburger. Peter tried not to outright drool at the sight of it, and the cardboard sleeve of fries reclining next to it. No food had ever looked so delicious. The fluorescent lights seemed to glint off every beckoning crystal of salt. He'd blown the last of his money on the boat ride to this little city by the sea and his last proper meal. Peter had always wanted to live by the ocean, and he figured now was the time to go for broke. *Well, congratulations*, he thought. *I sure am broke.* Peter had a pocketful of nickels and dimes. Nothing else. All those fifties spent on the bus, the hostel, those gorillas at the parking lot, the boat ride. In only seven days. *That must be some kind of record*, he smirked to himself. *Of patheticness.*

The kid crammed in a fistful of fries and chewed with his mouth open, watching Peter.

Peter turned his eyes back to his drawing. An instrumental version of the Foo Fighters' "Learn to Fly" came over the speakers. It was completely hideous. Peter started in on Birdie the Early Bird, who was dive-bombing the dragon with — uh-oh, could those be? — nuclear warheads. Nasty!

Finally, Eminem Boy wedged the last of his burger into his mouth with a backward thumb and started talking as he chewed. "Haven't seen you around before."

So that was it. A territory thing. There were plenty of people in the McDonald's, some of them probably dodging the rain same as him, but nobody was looking at the two of them. And nobody seemed particularly ready to stand up for a kid in stolen Wal-Mart clothes and a chewed-up haircut, either. Peter tensed and looked up from his drawing.

"No. I just came over on the boat this morning."

"Ferry."

Peter shot up in his seat, flexed his fists. "What did you say?"

The kid dropped his wrapper and held up his arms, palms out, like he was pushing against a wall. The friendliness switched off and his expression froze. Then he laughed, revealing more of the chew process than Peter really needed to see.

"*Ferry*. It's not called a boat. It's called a ferry." The smile he gave Peter was not something you could actually call warm. "It's really a, whaddyacallit, a ship, not a boat. Dekman told me that. *A ship is a boat that carries other boats.* But this one's called a ferry."

Peter rubbed his forehead once, twice, and nodded, although he had no idea what the kid was saying. Boats carrying boats? And what's a deck man? Trying for cool, he shrugged and let a moment pass while he said a silent farewell to the last of the fries off the kid's tray. He caught the eye of the girl behind the counter and quickly lowered his head. Get noticed and get thrown out. He was learning. Then he turned the question back on the kid. "Anyway, what are *you* doin'?"

This time, the smile seemed for real. "Nothin' much. But if you're done with your straw there, maybe I'll show you around a little."

There are two worlds out there, and if you're lucky — if your family is still together and nothing too terrible has happened to you, nothing too capital-T Tragic, like finding something at the back of a desk drawer that sets your soul to quaking, for example — then you've never seen this second world. Or maybe you have. Maybe you've walked down the main street of your city and right through the invisible line that divides your former life from this second world. If you have, you've seen a rare and terrible sight. And as hard as the vision is to acquire, you may well find someday that it's harder still to lose.

Peter grabbed his stuff and followed the kid out onto the sidewalk, giving the girl at the counter a shy smile on the way. No sense turning the staff against him. He'd be passing through those Golden Arches again, and maybe without a whole lot of quarters for Quarter Pounders to help the hours pass. The rain had stopped, but the leaves on the sad little trees that struggled to grow in their concrete planters drip-dripped. After the washing, the sky seemed brighter, cleaner. But still grey.

The two boys stood like that for a minute, blinking up at the new sky, Thursday shoppers elbowing past with their hands full of bags. Eminem Boy didn't speak, so Peter didn't speak right back at him. Was this it? Were they just going to stand there? They'd been inside. They'd been outside. Maybe those were the highlights of this town. Peter had immediately liked the downtown, the way the buildings were so small here, the towers ten storeys, tops. He liked the trees in their little metal cages on the sidewalk every twenty feet, even if the trees looked a little skeletal. He liked the variety of the people, not just suits and well-off window shoppers but all kinds of people. And they were actually walking. That was the first thing Peter had noticed about his latest city. Back home, nobody wandered the streets. Maybe because summers were so hot and winters so cold, nobody in their right mind spent more time on the sidewalk than they could help. It was a survival thing. But it seemed so much milder by the ocean. Even in the middle of November, Peter felt warm in the weak afternoon sunlight. And surrounded. Not so alone.

Still, he was starting to wonder why he and his new friend were just standing here, blocking the way into McDonald's. He tried drifting a little away from the door, but Eminem Boy didn't budge. Maybe the kid was waiting for his gang to come by and beat him into Peter McNuggets. His old life seemed very far away in that moment, especially Mary-Beth. He thought about the way he knew what she was thinking just from the look on her face, which was whatever the opposite of a poker face is, like a constantly updating computer readout. He missed the way he knew what to say to make the time pass, to make her laugh or make her mad, the way he could count on her for homework help and nutritious meal supplements. Right now, she seemed a million miles away. Peter's stomach growled. It sounded like the lion from the beginning of those movies.

"Hey," said an unfamiliar voice.

Two grimy kids had appeared out of nowhere, a boy and a girl. They smelled like wood smoke and B.O. "Hey," Eminem Boy answered.

The new kids both sported raggedy clothes and wary looks, but otherwise they were completely different from each other. The boy who'd spoken had a wicked case of acne, his cheeks like sausage meat let out of its bag, splotches of white and pink rippling across his face. He seemed unaware of his hideous complexion, but there was a challenge in every move he made.

His companion said nothing, though her body language did enough talking without her having to open her mouth. She bounced from one foot to the other, dancing a jig on the sidewalk like she had one finger in a wall socket. Every time she moved, dreadlocks flicked up into the clouds. She was tall and wore overalls, real mechanic's overalls with grease stains and a name tag that read MIKE. Peter thought she was pretty, then felt guilty for thinking that, then embarrassed about the whole thing.

"Hey," Hamburger Face barked again. He held a skate-board by his side. It was so long it came almost to his chest, which was something of an accomplishment. He was several inches taller than Peter and bent his head down to stare into Peter's eyes.

"Hey," Peter nodded. This wasn't so hard.

The two newcomers shot the first kid a questioning look.

"Guy's just off the ferry," Eminem Boy explained. "Thought I'd give him a little tour."

They eyed Peter, taking in the cuts and the bruising around his eye, the dirt, the smudges, the empty pack.

"Did you ask Dekman?"

"No. I just met him in there," the kid answered, thumbing back to the fast-food place. He sounded irritated. "But it said in my horoscope today *Change will come on the new wind*, and it sure was windy this morning. So I'm taking a break after the lunch rush and I go into Mickey D's for a minute and here's this kid drawing way-cool dragons and stuff, so I think maybe my horoscope's coming true." This was the longest speech Peter had heard from any of them yet. Even though it was only a few words, it took so long, with all the pauses to squint up and down the street and the interruptions from people struggling to get past them into

McDonald's for their own burger fix, that the hyper girl had skittered off altogether and was chasing pigeons out of doorways down the block.

Hamburger Face watched these antics for a minute, fiddled with something in one pocket, gnawed at a flap of skin on his lower lip, then turned to Peter again. "You got any money?"

"Umm…" Peter wasn't sure if this was a test or a transaction. "Not really. To be honest, I just spent my last dollar."

Neither boy seemed interested in this fact, and a stream of people flowed around the threesome as the sun finally broke through the clouds and lit up the street with an unreal clarity. The pavement began to steam. Peter's stomach made its hunting-on-the-savanna noise.

The girl zigzagged back toward them like she was under enemy fire. Her hair was in dreadlocks and the ropes snapped through the air like whips. Or snakes. *Medusa*, Peter remembered. Medusa was the monster woman with the snakes for hair. His fingers itched to draw this girl called Mike in the unlikely overalls, cobras or some sort of death-dealing viper wound around her skull in a poisonous crown, every part of her vibrating to some buzz just past human sensing.

"Hmph. Where you staying?"

"I don't know," Peter replied, trying to sound offhand,

like he knew the ropes, couldn't be bothered coming up with a plan but probably had one anyway. "Maybe the beach."

The trio burst out laughing. Hamburger Face thumped his skateboard. "Where are you *from*?" he asked. "You can't sleep there. The cops walk the beach all the time. You wanna get picked up?" Peter bit his tongue. He wasn't telling any more than he had to.

"Yeah," broke in the kid with the Eminem shirt, flipping back his long bangs. "You wanna end up at services?"

"Forget about it. He's clueless," the tall boy said. "Anyway, we're late."

He dropped his board and jumped on. The other two followed in his wake, the little one waggling a wave over one shoulder. The door between the worlds was swinging shut. Peter wasn't sure whether to feel sad or relieved.

The three were almost to the corner when they literally stopped in their tracks. The sidewalk was packed there with passengers stepping off a bus at the curb, but everyone cleared space for a strange apparition making its way toward Peter.

He was older than the three Peter had just met, nearly a grown-up. Peter instinctively understood he was in charge of them, and also that this was a situation he was used to. Apart from his height — he was taller than the others, even the crazy girl with the dreads — his most noticeable feature was a jester's hat in red and green. With every shake of his head, the points jangled with hidden bells. The rest of his clothes were almost as over-the-top: a T-shirt with PEEWEE FOR PRESIDENT and a picture of the disgraced entertainer, on top of shorts so long and wide Peter thought they were a skirt at first. Their frayed cuffs brushed the tops of mismatched high-tops in red and green, just like the hat.

He walked with confidence toward the McDonald's, not bothering to move out of anyone's way and not needing to. He let off a kind of intensity — and evil — that normal people seemed to pick up on instantly. They moved for him. Fast. The three kids Peter had been talking to rushed to follow in his wake and soon all five of them were standing in the doorway of the Golden Arches. Peter could see that the girl from behind the counter had been about to come out, but now she turned on her heel and retreated to her till. Nobody else seemed to feel the need to interrupt them either.

"Well, well. Having a little party, are we? And nobody thought to invite me?"

The youngest boy jumped over to the newcomer and whispered something in his ear. When he was done, the bells rang as the strange figure burst into more laughter. Passersby gave them surreptitious looks and sped past.

"So you're interested in marine life, eh? You'd like to become better acquainted with our delightful shores?" He checked to see how the other kids liked his joke. The girl with the overalls was halfway across the road by now, bouncing on some guy's bumper. He was yelling at her out his window, trying to protect his bald head with one hand as it started to rain again. She had her hands curled up under her armpits, hooting and scratching like a chimpanzee. None of the other kids even seemed to notice.

"What's your name, anyway, kid? What'd they used to call you?" His voice was deep, and gravelly.

"My name is Peter," he said, trying to sound equally grown-up and tough. "That's what they used to call me. And that's what they still call me."

Something about his tone seemed to bring the older boy up short and his eyes flicked wider. Blue with flecks of silver, Peter noticed, just like his own. A look of appraisal flashed across them. Peter had the strange feeling they'd met before, though he was sure that could not be true. This guy was not someone you could forget.

"Where'd you get those clothes, then, Peter?" He said Peter's name with a dismissive sneer. "How come they're so new and fancy if you don't have money? And where'd you get that haircut? *Just off the boat?* I don't think so." He turned to include the two kids beside Peter and the girl now turning cartwheels down the sidewalk. He raised his voice against the traffic.

"He's a narc, you morons! I had to come all the way down here to tell you that?" He lowered the volume slightly, then bent toward Peter, his bells brushing the top of Peter's head. "You're a narc, one of Carruthers' special boys slumming with the gutter trash, looking for crumbs. Well, no thanks, Peter Peter Pumpkin Eater. We're not interested."

He whistled to the boy with the zits, who had darted into the road to argue with another teenager who was holding a squeegee and yelling in a strong Spanish accent, and called, "See ya 'round, narc!" Hamburger Face turned reluctantly away from the squeegee boy and joined their group just as another bus pulled up to the stop and spewed out another load of people.

The foursome ran through the crowd and vanished around a corner. On the afternoon breeze, Peter heard the echo of two final sounds, a drawn-out "N-a-a-a-arc" and the mocking jangle of bells.

Two young mothers glared at Peter as they finally made it through the doors of McDonald's and back outside, pushing their umbrella strollers in front of them. Peter stuck his hands in his empty pockets and swept his eyes up and down the rutted concrete surface of the road. Everything seemed so normal now. It was like the scene with those strange kids had never happened. Like that weird circus girl hadn't been doing acrobatics down this very sidewalk just seconds ago. The street was full of cars and buses again. The sidewalk had its share of regular folk going about their business. The stores on this block were like stores on any block. He could be back home, on his way to Neon Peon. Then he happened to catch a reflection of himself in a store window — bedraggled, the black outfit, the sticking-out hair. Yes, the street was normal, the people were normal, but he was not. It was time to move on.

Maybe the beach wasn't the best choice, Peter had to admit. It had been hours since his last meal on the boat — ferry — that had brought him here and he felt sharp pains now in his gut every time he thought about food. Which was every three seconds. Tops. The oceanfront was windy and each gust brought in another damp blast of sea. So far from streetlights, the ground was lit only by the pale glow of the new moon. He'd been here a couple hours already and figured it was now close to midnight. Far down the curve of the shore, Peter thought he saw the dance of fires in the darkness. Spooky. Even though it looked dorky, even though it symbolized a whole other life, he regretted chucking his parka. The move had seemed defiant that day in the park, but on this cold November night, it seemed more than a little short-sighted. He drew the hood of his sweatshirt tight around his head and tucked his arms up inside the sleeves. His ears felt cold without the old covering of hair. He missed his hair.

Plus, the brat had been right: the cops had come by — twice. The first time just to give the place a once-over, the second to make a careful search among the logs and driftwood. When they came back, they each carried a two-foot-long flashlight, and that time the bright beams hadn't hesitated to pick out Peter, hunched in the lee of a boulder. The policemen clearly hadn't believed his story about a class project on stargazing, and they'd made him promise he wouldn't be there when they returned in an hour. They looked bored as they outlined his options: go home or go in for holding overnight. Business as usual for them, Peter figured.

He had no idea whether they really would return, or where he could go instead. A dozen times he made to leave, thinking he could kill the hours till dawn walking the neighbourhoods around the waterfront. The idea of calling his mom even got him up onto his feet. If he still had his father's money he could be inside now, warm and safe. His mind kept returning to those three goons from the bus.

He knew they'd probably blown the cash already and some-how that made the insult worse. Goddamn country punks. He spent some time wishing them highly detailed, painful deaths.

His mother had been right about one thing. He couldn't be trusted to hang on to it.

Had she got his message? He had to admit that he missed her. He missed Mary-Beth, the old street, his friends. But to go back didn't even feel possible anymore. He'd crossed a line somewhere. Maybe out in that truck stop parking lot. Or in the bathroom with the scissors. Or maybe over an empty cup in a fast-food joint.

As he watched the moonlight pick out the tops of the whitecaps, Peter felt the day's strains sink in. He'd never had to think about basics like food and shelter before. And on top of that, he had no idea what to do about the letter he'd found, the adoption paper. *Not* thinking about it was even more wearing than just getting it over with. Was the letter the key to a new life? Peter's mind jumped to a crazy thought: another family out there, a man and woman searching for him too, desperate to swing time around and slot him into their perfect prefab lives.

Was the news even really so bad? Maybe he'd massively overreacted. Every kid dreams at some point that he discovers his whole life is a sham, that his real parents —

astronauts, royalty, secret agents — have a better life to offer their long-lost child. That isn't such a bad fantasy. But fantasy is all it is, usually. Peter tried to feel lucky, tried to feel the world had opened up instead of shutting down, but failed. Besides, it wasn't just about the adoption. The two of them had kept this secret from him for fourteen years, the most basic fact of Peter's life tucked neatly into the furthest reaches of a desk drawer. What else wasn't real? What else was a lie?

In spite of his anxieties and the cold, Peter was exhausted. The steady shush of sea was like the voice of the hypnotist urging, "Sleep ... sleep ... sleep ..." He struggled to stay alert, fearful that the cops might reappear at any moment. In fact, he had this feeling he was being watched. There were eyes on him somewhere. It occurred to him that at least the police station would be heated. He'd trust to fate. Crouched down against a boulder, his skinny black arms wrapped around his sodden black knees, Peter slept.

At some point, he found himself dreaming a world of white again. The white of the ground and the white of the sky flowed into that same unmeasured emptiness — no beginning, no end, no hot or cold, bright or dark. Part of his waking mind recalled his last dream in the park near the hostel. He struggled to remember whether this dream was safe or not. He had a memory of panic, but he was distracted by the whiteness itself. It was almost sticky, like spider's silk. He felt cradled by it, safe. Less worried about where his own body ended and the whiteness began. It felt familiar and soothing. There was a sound this time, so distant it was almost beyond hearing. In his dream-mind he turned this way and that, trying to locate the source. Then he realized the buzz, a low hum like the way his father's speakers sounded when the stereo first came on, was part of the nothing itself. Peter was surrounded by an electrical whiteness. The sound was holding the world at a distance, just like the nothingness had before. Again, Peter felt like he was separated from his troubles, like he was standing in a hallway and all his worries had been helpfully moved into rooms behind locked doors. He could just make out their shadowy outlines behind the whiteness, could just hear those troubles calling to him from beneath the unearthly hum. *Can I just leave them behind?* Peter wondered. With that, he woke up.

The sky was growing lighter, though the sun was still an hour or so away. Assuming he'd arrived about ten, that meant nine long hours on the cold sand. No wonder he felt so chilled and sore. His sneakers were soaked with dew and crusted with sand. A thick paste of yesterday's fast food and new morning hunger coated the inside of his mouth. Coughing, he could see his breath in the predawn air.

As he creaked to stand, a scrap of paper fluttered to his feet. Peter snagged it. It looked like a business card. Peter tilted it in the dim light to pick out black letters:

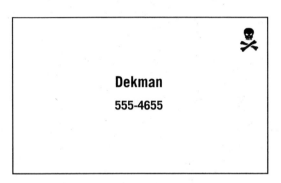

That *was what the kid with the Eminem shirt had said. Not deck man. Dekman.*

A name. A phone number. In one corner, a ballpoint drawing of a skull and crossbones. His skin prickled with fear. Or premonition. Peter scanned the beach, trying to determine where it could have come from, but the sand was deserted. He was alone.

CHAPTER SIX

A block from the beach Peter found a pay phone outside a twenty-four-hour animal hospital. He could hear a dog howling. Ellen or Jester Boy. Which one? He'd promised his mother he'd call. In fact, he was a day late. But he didn't feel up to it.

He wasn't sure he'd ever feel up to it.

Either number would at least satisfy some kind of curiosity. He snagged the envelope from his back pocket and pulled out the single piece of paper inside. The feeling that he was being watched hadn't completely disappeared but a quick scan said all was clear. Peter unfolded the sheet and read again the few lines it contained: his parents' names, his place of birth, the date. There was nothing to show who his real parents were, no name or address, just a stamp of a signature at the bottom, and a file number. What was he supposed to do with that? What good was a piece of paper that told him something so huge and so useless at the same time? Why even bother handing around pieces of paper like this? If only Mary-Beth were here: she was the writer in the outfit, the researcher, the snoop. Peter was more into the big picture. Pictures in general. He was a decent artist and could be creative when it came to solving problems, but it was Mary-Beth who knew how to lay down the steps to get from beginning to end. Details were her thing. But then, it could be argued her not being here was kind of the point.

Peter's stomach rumbled: he'd have to figure out how to get food soon. He had in total one quarter and he knew he should spend it on something responsible like sesame snacks or a banana or something, but right now he was hungrier for answers than for food. He folded away the baffling document and fished out the unexplained business card instead. His fingers moved on their own, slotted the coin, started dialing.

The phone rang and rang, but nobody picked up. Terrific. Peter slammed down the receiver. Tried again. Nope. Here he was, friendless, starving, desperate, then a phone number materializes out of thin air and it's no more helpful than the stupid adoption form. Somebody had played a joke on him, and he'd fallen for it. He was such a loser. Yesterday's tough-guy 'tude was gone.

Peter turned again to check the street. It was early still, few cars or people out. But he couldn't shake the feeling that someone was watching him.

Think, Peter ordered himself. *Think this through.* His father had always told him the trick to being a good lawyer was patience. Law didn't take brains, really, or any special skills. It just took patience and concentration. "You reduce the possibilities until only one course of action remains," Jack would explain, like it was the easiest thing in the world. And maybe it was — for his dad. Turned out that was another skill he couldn't hope to inherit.

Peter dropped to the sidewalk and stuck his damp feet out into the weak morning sun. At this rate, they should be dry just in time for the next rainstorm. He picked at some dried crud on the leg of his new jeans, checked his watch for the millionth time, squinted into the distance.

Okay, Dad. Possibilities. You want to talk possibilities? He flicked out his thumb.

One: The card wasn't meant for him. The wind had blown it across the beach and it just landed on him. Unlikely, he had to admit. What were the chances he'd meet this Dekman character one day and find his card the next?

Two: The cops put it there. But why? To warn him? To threaten him? If so, couldn't they have just said their piece when they were giving him his options? Were they trying to recruit him? *Slumming with the gutter trash,* Peter remembered. *Looking for crumbs.*

Three: Somebody else put it there. Like, somebody Peter didn't even know, somebody who'd seen him with the kids downtown. This was weird but possible. It would explain the spidey sense that someone had been watching him since he'd got off the ferry.

Four: The card did come from that kid with the hat, from Dekman, but he'd changed his mind. That's why nobody answered the phone: he'd made the offer — what, was not exactly clear — then thought better of it. Now he was going to ignore him until Peter got the hint.

Peter looked at his thumb sticking up, his fingers stretched out like a little kid's pretend gun. He straightened his pinkie.

Five: The guy genuinely wanted to help. Peter stood, scooped the quarter from the coin return, and studied it. "Well," he said, "let's reduce some possibilities." And he slotted it again.

"Do you always talk to yourself?"

Peter dropped the receiver and whirled around. There on the sidewalk was the hyper girl from downtown. Her hair was in pigtails this morning and she wore a red Chinese dress with a huge gold dragon wrapped around it. She looked like she'd just stepped out of an MTV video. "You should see your face!"

"What are you doing here?"

"What am *I* doing here? Maybe I own this sidewalk. Maybe I'm just heading out for my morning — what do you call it — my morning constitutional. Maybe I'm on my paper route. What are *you* doing here? Isn't it a little on the early side to be making phone calls?" She smiled sweetly and, honest to God, batted her eyelashes. *Bat-bat.* Peter felt faint, and for once it had nothing to do with missing food groups.

He looked up and down the street again. Fittingly, it was called Beach Drive. One side was nothing but sand and sea. The other boasted mostly low-rise apartment buildings, their windows curtained against the almost dawn, and a forlorn mini mall. Nothing moved in any direction. His watch said 7:15. It *was* a little on the early side. Say what you like about homelessness, it sure gets you going in the morning. If his mother could only see him now.

He tried not to show how rattled he felt. "I don't think you're allowed to own sidewalks."

"Smart guy. So, do you?"

Peter gave a blank face.

"Always talk to yourself?"

The girl dropped into a fair imitation of those Russian dancers who cross their arms and kick out their legs while crouching just above the ground. The effect was all the more surreal with the dragon dress and the combat boots.

"If there's nobody else worth talking to."

"But you were phoning someone. Who was it? Mommy to come pick you up?"

Peter blushed, like she could read his mind, then righted himself. "I was just calling ... a friend. But he's not awake yet, I guess."

The girl nodded and stretched her arms out into an enormous yawn. Right on cue, the sun broke free of the horizon behind her, silhouetting her graceful pose. "Oh. I thought you were calling Dekman. That's why I gave you the card."

Her name was Cat, and she'd known Dekman six months. She gave a smirk when she said it, like he could take whatever he liked from that statement. Peter instantly became tongue-tied, and concentrated on how intoxicating his bacon tasted after a night on a soggy beach. Better than any drug, Cat agreed. She seemed so at home in this deserted diner at the back end of a strip mall miles from downtown facing the sea, Peter wondered if maybe she lived nearby. Although she didn't smell like someone who lived any-where with a regular hygiene routine. She was sixteen. She said.

"So why did you give me that card really?"

"Because Dekman told me to." Cat shrugged and bounced up. She ran behind the counter and scooped up a handful of jam packets. Back in the booth, she spread the jam across a triangle of toast. She had a very particular technique, which required tiny dollops on the tip of her knife. She vigorously massaged the jam in small circles into each section of toast. Peter had never seen such a deliberate and pointless approach to food preparation.

"But why?"

"Why? Why what? Why did I give you the card? I told you. Because Dekman told me to. He said that if you really spent the night at the beach, if you didn't get all buddy-buddy with the cops, if the J squad didn't drop by, I should give you the card. I almost checked out when I saw the pair with the flashlights, but then you got the speech that everybody gets — man, those cops talk loud! — so then I started thinking maybe you were okay." She fixed him with a serious stare, then beat a complicated drum solo onto the chipped edge of the table with her knife. It seemed to have very little to do with the music on the radio, whatever it was. Simon and Garfunkel, that was it. Old-school hippie stuff. Strawberry drops rained down out of time to the beat. "Maybe," she repeated.

Peter wasn't sure if this was a compliment, but he remembered his manners and swallowed his retort. She was the one buying breakfast, after all. He opened his mouth to ask another question, but Cat beat him to it.

"Why did Dekman want to give you the card? How should I know?" Cat yelled this last line, and Peter looked with embarrassment around the diner. But at this hour, they were the only customers. "How many people does Dekman give his card to? Why did I do what Dekman asked me to do? How could I possibly stand to hang around all night watching you pick your nose by moonlight? That's too long a story for breakfast. Why is there air?" The whole thing was becoming embarrassing, so Peter tried to go on the offensive.

"I could have been phoning the cops that very second you came up to me by the beach. How did you know I wasn't?"

"Kid," she said with a laugh. "You know that expression 'face like an open book'? They were thinking of you when they invented it."

Peter flashed back to Mary-Beth, to the way he always teased her that she couldn't keep a secret if she tried, and scowled. He wasn't like that. He slurped up the last of his tea and desperately struggled to think of a way to change the topic.

"Why is he called that, anyway? What kind of a name is Dekman? Or Cat, for that matter?"

"Kid. Peter. Whatever. I just give you the card, make sure you are who you say you are, and get some food into you. That's my job. Anything else you need, you ask Dekman the next time you see him."

"When will—"

Before Peter could finish, she'd spun out of the booth, dropped some bills on the table, and was out the door.

The waitress came out from the back with a teapot and approached Peter's table. Together they watched the red-clad figure hightail it out of the parking lot. The waitress shook her head as she refilled his chipped mug.

"I'd like to know what she's always in such an all-fired hurry for, anyway." Without waiting for an answer, she scooped up the money and disappeared the way she'd come.

Peter looked across the tableful of jam and sighed. Alone again.

During the endless morning and afternoon, between trying to reach Dekman (no answer, busy, no answer) and trying to screw up the courage to call Ellen, Peter had plenty of time to think over the events of the past few days. He was shocked to realize that just over a week had passed since the fight with Alex and the trip to the lawyer's. His dad had been dead for two weeks, and already his life was unrecognizable.

Peter suspected he was acting out of control. But then, he asked himself, how are you supposed to act when you lose half your family only to discover it's not even your real family anyway? His reaction had been to get into a fight, run away from home, get into another fight, lose $400, start shoplifting, and sleep on the beach. A little extreme, maybe, but not all that whacked given the crazy things that had happened to him. Maybe a normal kid would go into therapy, wash down his Coco-Puffs with Ritalin, lose himself in extra trigonometry ... but if that was normal, Peter wanted none of it.

He remembered when he was in Grade 5 or 6 hearing about a kid in his school whose parents had both died in some freak accident. This kid, who had probably been in Grade 10, had gone way crazier. One morning he drove into the school parking lot in a brand-new Lotus Spider. None of the kids had seen anything like it, and everyone crowded around. The boy, who was barely old enough to drive, didn't even seem that proud, although it was an insanely powerful car. Kids were whispering that his parents had died and he'd blown the inheritance. Later, the word was he'd totalled the car and dropped out of school. Peter had heard the story thirdhand from a friend's older brother and didn't even remember the kid's name. He was just the Lotus Spider kid with the dead parents.

Seen from this perspective, his own little "vacation" didn't seem that out-of-line. The main thing, Peter decided, was to make the most of life before something precious gets broken, like it inevitably will. It just didn't seem possible that life would improve if he called his mom and she offered him bus fare home.

His mother had a different opinion.

He'd finally called right after lunch — at least, the time people call lunch when they have access to food in the middle of the day — and she'd picked up on the first ring.

"Peter! Oh, thank God! Where are you?"

"Mom. Please, don't panic. I'm fine."

"Fine? Peter! Do you realize how worried I've been? Nobody's seen you. Nobody knows where you are. I kept imagining you were ... Where are you staying? Mary-Beth says she doesn't know where you are but if I find out you've been staying with her, I'll be livid, Peter. Livid. The Kennedys have enough to deal with without having to take care of you as well."

"Mom. Listen to me. I'm not staying at Mary-Beth's."

"Well, tell me where you are, then. I'll come pick you up."

Peter thought of the clothes he'd dumped, the backpack. He thought of his old mousy hair.

"Mom, you can't pick me up where I am. But that's not important. Mom, I found an envelope. In Dad's study, hidden way at the back of one of his desk drawers. It said—"

"Oh, Peter. Stop right there. This isn't something to talk about over the telephone. Your father and I agreed that when the time was right, we'd all sit down and discuss it like civilized people. Please, honey, tell me where you are. I'm …" A moment of silence hummed with electrons rolling down the wires and across the country. A harried-looking businessman took out his cellphone right next to Peter and started talking into it, like this was the phone zone. "Oh, Peter. When I came home to the house all empty, your things gone …"

She took another tack. "Honey, of course you're upset. This is natural. But I'm asking you to be sensible and come back home so we can talk properly. Just tell me where you are and I can help."

Peter could almost see Ellen on the kitchen extension, standing by the windows that looked out over the back yard, cord stretched over the dining table. She was using the voice his dad called her volunteer voice. "God save us from the volunteer voice," Jack would say during a fight, when Ellen was being stubbornly reasonable. "Just yell it out, Ellen. Don't condescend to me!"

Anger sparked. "Sensible? You want me to be sensible, Mom? My father just died. I don't feel like being sensible. Plus you lied to me. You've lied to me my entire life. You and Dad. And now you want me to be sensible? To be civilized and polite and … and … and … I don't think so."

"Peter Weir. You listen to me—"

"No! I'm sick of listening." He slammed down the phone and cut himself off from the only home he'd ever known.

CHAPTER SEVEN

Peter felt stupid holding the sign, but Dekman hadn't given him a lot of choice.

"People don't give money 'cause it's fun to give," Dekman had said. "They give money because they can't come up with a reason not to fast enough."

Peter had no idea what this meant, but he'd nodded. It seemed best to agree.

"So you take a piece of cardboard and you write something on it. Something funny. People laugh, they feel good, they give you a dollar. It's easy."

"And then what?"

"And then what, what?"

"And then what do I do? How long do I have to sit here?"

"Who bought you breakfast this morning? And dinner last night? How you gonna afford lunch in a few hours, bright boy? I'll tell you how long you have to sit here. Till I tell you not to." Dekman had been all business this morning, no more bells or high-tops. He wore a T-shirt with POST-DATE THE STATE scribbled on it in black pen, plus black jeans and boots. And his head, no longer hidden under the jester's hat, was a shaved skull. Narrow and mean. The only relief was a pair of silver hoops through his ears and a sandy-brown Vandyke. He looked like Rob Zombie's younger brother.

"Spike'll come by at lunch and see what you've got. Don't screw up and don't steal my money." Spike, it turned out, was the one with the hamburger face. "Or you will be hurt."

"What about the cops?"

"The cops? The cops are the last thing you should worry about."

Then he'd just stood up and walked away. Farther down the block, a bunch of kids were gathered around a German shepherd on the sidewalk. Dekman went up to them and started whooping at the dog, which set it to barking loudly. The whole group laughed and disappeared around a corner.

Peter had been so busy watching Dekman he hadn't noticed Eminem Boy, the first kid he'd met, emerge from the shadows of the doorway behind him.

"Hey."

"Hey," Peter nodded. The kid's name, Cat had told him, was Thumper. When he poured on the angel charm, he could get coin from a dead man, she'd said, but he was too lazy for his own good. That was cold. Peter wondered what she would say about him. Maybe nothing yet.

"Whassup?" Thumper asked. "This your corner now?"

"I guess so. Dekman told me not to move. He told me I have to do a sign or something." Peter felt like an idiot even saying the words.

"Yeah, he made me do that too." He stared hard at Peter for a long minute, then patted the pockets of his army surplus coat. Frowning, he looked up and down the street, then brightened. "Stay here." He reached back into the coat and pulled out a copy of *Heavy Metal* magazine. "Here, read this till I get back. Don't lose it!"

He pasted his long blond bangs behind his ears and stood up straight. He'd gone from dirty and threatening to dirty but respectable. And he looked even younger, if that was possible, as he sauntered across the street and into the convenience store on the corner.

He returned in a few minutes, whistling as he checked

both ways before crossing. Hunched down beside Peter, he pulled a pack of markers out of the waistband of his fatigues. Peter opened his eyes wide and Thumper blushed with pride.

He still felt dumb, even though the sign did make people laugh. And Dekman was right. Peter had to give him that. He was clearly all over the crowd psychology. When they laughed, they dropped a coin or two. Not many actual dollars, but the dimes and quarters added up too. And the sign had been fun to make. He'd done the letters in that barbed-wiry German writing that was on the cover of *Heavy Metal* magazine: WHO'S YOUR TAILOR? QUASIMODO? A *Roger Rabbit* line, though probably nobody but him would get that. He'd done it for Thumper, to say thanks for the markers without being all girly about it, and the fun of inking the letters made him realize how happy art made him. Art class was the one place where he felt like everyone spoke a language he understood. Peter zoned through a lot of school, but never art.

Around the middle of the day, which, thankfully, had been dry even though he was freezing his butt on November cement, Spike came by with a slice of pizza and a Coke for him. He didn't count Peter's earnings, but he did give a grunt before he dropped the money into his pocket. It was a Saturday, and the people wandering the streets were out for early Christmas shopping. Lucky for Peter, they were feeling the holiday spirit nice and early. Peter was debating whether to ask what was supposed to happen next, but by the time he opened his mouth, Spike had already skated off.

Peter thought he should be angry. After all, he'd been sitting on this stupid piece of sidewalk for what felt like three hundred hours and Spike hadn't even said one word to him. He'd taken all his money — Peter could have bought his own pizza and Coke with that change — and who knew what was supposed to happen next. On the other hand, nobody had bothered him, and he suspected Dekman had something to do with that.

He remembered his first day off the boat. Ferry. Whatever. He'd felt like everybody's eyes were on him. First all the little old ladies. Then, because of the extreme makeover in the mall, the kids from the street. Even Thumper had given him the once-over that first day. And the cops on the beach with their flashlight clubs. But now, protected by nothing but a cardboard sign and, he assumed, a word from Dekman, things were under control. Kind of. For the first time in weeks, Peter felt a stirring of something he couldn't name. He wasn't hungry. He was cold, but he probably wouldn't die from it. He had something to do, even if it was stupid, and people he knew a little. It wasn't even raining. There was a word for it, and he laughed when it hit him. He was happy.

The day was still long. Long, like double English followed by double English followed by double English. Plus detention. Thumper dropped by again and produced a chocolate bar from one of the zillion zippered pockets on the sides of his pants and read him his horoscope. Nothing good: *Weather the storm, count your blessings, bide your time.* Later, Cat waved as she walked past with a group of kids Peter hadn't seen before. Otherwise, he held up the sign, thanked people for the change, and squirmed on the hard cement to try to bring some life back into his rear.

It felt like a lifetime. He stood and stretched a lot, trying to ease out the soreness from sitting all day and from having slept in a huge park at the edge of the city. Cat had taken him there the night before, checking over her shoulder before pointing to a sort of cave protected by the thick leaves of the strangest plant Peter had ever seen, broad-leafed and hairy, like something from the time of the dinosaurs.

"You can sleep here for tonight. It doesn't look like much, but it's better than the beach, trust me. It's dry from the leaves. And warm. At the back it bumps up against the petting zoo. See? The animals inside give off a lot of heat. And best of all, no cops."

Peter had raised his eyes and wrinkled his nose at the combination of Cat and petting zoo in close quarters, but said nothing. He was learning.

The cave had been warm and dry, just like Cat promised, even if there was quite the stench. The longer Peter spent on the streets, the less he cared about that. When he was inside, watching the last of the sun bounce off the grass just outside the entrance, it reminded him of hideouts from when he was a little kid. When his parents had the neighbours over at Christmas, or parties for one of Ellen's volunteer groups, he'd crouch under the dining table, peeking out from under the tablecloth, listening to the grown-ups talk about the weather and waiting for someone to realize he was missing.

Well, people knew he was missing now. That was for sure. It wouldn't make his dad come back. He knew that. It wasn't like it was a comfort or anything — life, like the hard ground underneath him now, wasn't comfortable.

If Mary-Beth could see him now.

The long day was done. Peter felt bored when the stores shook themselves free of their little shoppers like a dog getting rid of its fleas. There was a wave of them all at once, everybody bent on getting home with their shiny new shinies, followed by a trickle of overachievers spending Saturday at the office. They didn't have silver for Peter. They didn't even make eye contact. It was like part of them was already in their kitchen deciding what to make for dinner. Peter wondered what would happen next. He hoped Cat might come by, or Thumper.

A few minutes later, he heard the rhythmic whir-slap of a skateboard, like a photocopier on overdrive. He looked around. So far, all the skaters he'd encountered knew Dekman.

"Hey," Spike called down to Peter. His board was modified to swivel at both axles and he was constantly pulling these huge pop shove-its and other cool tricks. Off the board, he seemed a lot less interesting.

"Hey," Peter nodded. He was down with the routine and rose stiffly to hand the afternoon's haul to Spike. This time, the other boy actually counted the money and rolled his eyes.

"Dekman said to feed you. How can I feed you on this?" He sighed and craned his head around Peter, scanning the street for options. "Let's go."

Spike ollied up the sidewalk through the last of the thinning crowds. As he followed, Peter's stomach clenched with the promise of protein.

They ended up at a twenty-four-hour Chinese dive called The Tin Shoe, with harsh fluorescent lighting, tureens of won ton soup, and a scattering of people sitting alone at tables covered in plastic sheets, waiting for the daily specials.

As they ate, Peter tried to pump Spike for information. He'd had a lot of hours to think about everything and he was starting to see some connections.

"You work for Dekman, right?" he asked. "Like, Dekman is your boss and you guys all work for him."

"I don't work for Dekman," Spike laughed. "I don't work for nobody. I'm a free spirit. An independent contractor. I could walk tomorrow if I wanted to."

"Walk from where?" Peter asked.

"From … Dekman. From all this," the boy answered, sweeping his arms to take in the room.

"So why don't you? What's so great about Dekman?"

"You'll see," Spike answered. "Maybe." He seemed to think better of the conversation and finished his meal quickly and deliberately, head down. Peter felt frustrated that nobody would just tell him what was going on, but he was relieved when Spike left abruptly without another word. Spike's face wasn't exactly good for the appetite.

The next day, a Sunday, was a repeat of the previous day. Breakfast: doughnuts and coffee. Lunch: pizza and Coke. Dinner: Tin Shoe. Another night camping in the park, sleep disturbed by the whiteouts that were becoming as much a routine as every part of his strange new life. Peter pulled in a few handfuls of change from passing shoppers, nothing big, though one guy gave him two bucks because he liked the sign of the day. This one featured a cartoon image of Peter behind bars, like in that old Elvis movie on TV every other weekend. Out of the cartoon Peter's mouth came a balloon that read SINCE MY BABY LEFT ME.

But the price for the two bucks was completely not worth it. He had to listen to the guy sing the entire song, cupping his cellphone like some Vegas lounge singer. Peter had thought he'd hit bottom, but it seemed there was always lower to go.

There was no sign of Dekman that day. And after dinner, again in the delightful and attractive company of the morose Spike, Peter asked if there was ever going to be any news.

"I'm getting a little bored sitting out there," he said. Spike jerked his head out of his noodles, obviously about to deliver a lecture. Peter threw up his hands in a calming gesture. "Which is fine, really. But it gives me all this time to, you know, wonder. Like, what's happening. I'm handing over the money, you guys are feeding me a delicious and satisfying range of meals featuring all four food groups. And I'm grateful. Really." Peter rushed through the rest to get it out of the way. Band-Aids are always better pulled off quickly. "But what's the deal? You don't sleep under a bush in the park, Spike. You don't sit on your butt all day holding a cardboard sign. How come I have to?"

Spike pushed the last greasy forkfuls of pork around his plate and spread out his hands. Big sigh. "Dekman says life is about trust. As in, don't. Dekman says don't trust anyone and you won't be disappointed."

The waitress arrived and dropped the bill and two fortune cookies onto the table. Spike took the bigger cookie without even bothering to look at Peter. Peter cracked his and read aloud: "A new project will lead to great rewards." Spike leaned across the remains of their meal and snorted, "They're so full of it." He read his own silently, swore, then crumpled it into a ball and dropped it onto his plate.

"Dekman will tell you when it's time. The Dekman never forgets."

Spike drained his Coke, stood up and skated right out of the restaurant to a barrage of yelling from the waitress about leaving skateboards outside.

Alone again. Peter reached across the table and fished the soggy fortune out of the grease on Spike's plate. It read: *Trouble finds a way when the door is left open.*

The following morning it was back to raining and for a few minutes Peter lay in his leafy hideout and pretended he was still home, listening to the patter on the skylight of his attic room. He imagined it was Sunday. He could almost hear the ritual noises of his parents fixing a weekend breakfast, the grinding of the coffee beans and the whir of the espresso machine, the ka-thunk! of the toaster, the steady whump of the fridge door opening and closing, opening and closing. The sounds were so cozy and familiar.

You'll never win friends and influence people hiding under a bush, he told himself. With a grunt, he laboured up onto his sore feet and out into the sodden park. The world waited. New projects for a new week. Great rewards.

But first, a shower. Thumper had taken him aside the day before and explained that if he wanted to smell like that, well, that was Peter's business. But stinking that bad was not ideal for business. Thumper ripped a band poster off a telephone pole and drew Peter a map of downtown on the back. Important places got stars. Trouble spots got a death's head. Right in the middle was an arrow and "Peter goes here and stops stinking."

"Just go to the drop-in centre and tell them you're thinking about going back to school. Then they got to give you a free shower and maybe some food — if there's any left."

The drop-in centre was clean and friendly and made Peter feel even more like an outcast than he already did. He got the shower, and the lecture. It was embarrassing. Begging was fine. Being handed a threadbare towel by a pretty social worker and pointed to the shower was, well, brutal. No thanks. He swore he'd never go back, even though the building was on the way from the park to his spot downtown.

There was no dry cardboard in the alleys by the time he got to his usual spot, and he hadn't thought to save something to write on, so he was forced to talk. At first, he was full of wisecracks, but as the hours passed with no sign of kids or lunch he fell into a bad mood. He'd snagged his hoodie on something, and cold seeped in through the tear. To pass the time, he tried to figure out the meaning of the dreams he kept having. After that second one at the beach, they were showing up every night. None of them were as long or as overwhelming as that one had been, but night after night, he found himself inside that whiteness. Like a corridor. Alone. Invisible. Not scared anymore, but unnerved, definitely, by the haze and the hum. That was all there ever was. White light. White noise. It was all so baffling. The suddenness of it, the helplessness. When it would start. Where it would lead.

As he considered the sensation of it, he began to wonder if maybe the whiteness was not a destination at all. Maybe that blank feeling, that nothingness, was just a beginning, not an end. He decided that next time he found himself in that dream, he wouldn't struggle. He'd try to move *through* it. "Like a video game," he muttered to himself. "Try to get to the next level."

People walked by. Office workers. Mothers. Crazy old people. A few times the cops. Most gave him a pious little shake of the head, a few added a bit of currency. As his mood blackened and his back started spasming from the uncomfortable concrete, he lost it. Instead of polite please and thank-you's, he began yelling the worst reasons possible for why he needed money. Business picked up immediately.

"Money for drugs!" *Clink.*

"Money for personal grooming products!" *Clink.*

"Money for Satan." *Clink.*

"Money to make my pockets go clink-clink!" *Clink-clink.*

Life was truly ridiculous.

A guy in a jacket and tie leaned against a nearby store-front, watching him, listening to the dropping coins and the various pitches.

"Money for freedom. Money for freedom-fighting weaponry." *Clink.*

The suit smiled and nodded to himself. He came closer, squatted down, and pulled a twenty out of a leather wallet. He held it by one corner, then gently placed it in Peter's cup.

Peter looked at the bill, looked up at the man, then sucked in his breath. Under the grey fedora, he saw Dekman's smirking Vandyke.

"Very nice, Peter. Very nice. I think things are going to work out after all. Call me at five."

After several days spent imagining exactly what Dekman would say and what Peter would say back and how impressed Dekman would be by Peter's street-savvy style, all Peter could actually do was gape as Dekman stood, brushed the dust of the streets from his pressed trousers, and unfurled an umbrella. As he picked his way through the crowd, Dekman turned and called back to Peter: "Now, don't you spend that all in one place, young man!"

CHAPTER EIGHT

Five on the nose and Peter was back at a pay phone dropping another of his hard-earned quarters into the slot. An image rushed into his head of kids all around the city working as slaves to the pay phone gods, their lives nothing but a way to circulate quarters from one hulking machine to the next. It was like a drawing in his mind, him and all the other street kids like worker ants, carrying little balls of coins to their queens. Creepy. The ring in his ear snapped him back to the present.

Pick up ...

Dekman's number was a cell, and Peter wondered for the millionth time what the deal was with this weird man-child.

Who hands out business cards to street kids?

The line clicked and a voice came on against a shrieking sound, like a metal monster being put through a high-speed grinder.

Dekman's voice rode over top of the racket and straight into Peter's ear.

"This is Peter. Good. At nine o'clock you'll be standing outside the place where we first met. Do you remember?"

"Yes," Peter yelled to make himself heard. "I remember."

"Don't be late. And don't be early. Nine o'clock."

The line went dead, and in the sudden silence, it took a few seconds for the normal sounds of the street to register again. Peter checked the coin return out of habit, then his watch. Three and three-quarter hours. He went back to his corner and waited twenty minutes, but he had the feeling nobody was coming to take him out for dinner today. He was on his own, at least until nine. He figured the money he'd collected, including Dekman's twenty, was his, so he left his corner and started wandering. He didn't really have a destination in mind, but he figured that inevitably he'd wind up at the mall. It was destiny, he figured.

He'd gone about two blocks when he heard yelling. Well, not yelling but very loud speechifying. Preacher Sal, it had to be. Peter rounded the corner and sure enough, there the old man was outside the Roundabout Records shop.

Everybody who lived on the street knew Preacher Sal. Summer and winter he pushed his buggy up and down the alleys and side streets and into the loading bays of all the office buildings. He looked like your classic homeless guy, tall and gaunt with long stringy hair and a hawk-like nose. He reminded Peter of a character from an old ocean movie, *Moby-Dick*, the one who tries to warn the hero guy not to board the whaling ship. But the hero won't listen. Death and mayhem follow, of course. What's new?

Most of the kids gave Preacher Sal a wide berth. Peter had too, at first, hanging back while the guy lectured anyone in earshot, but already he was realizing that there was an intelligence there — the 52-pick-up kind, sure, ideas all over the place, but intelligence nonetheless. Sal was the only person who showed any real interest in Peter in those early days, for one thing, even if that interest wasn't exactly consistent. (Dekman didn't count; Dekman was a mystery.) Preacher Sal was a gentle person, as long as you didn't argue with him. Argue with him and he could get riled up. That was one of Dekman's favorite pastimes. For Dekman, Preacher Sal was like a firecracker: he wasn't any fun unless you lit him up and set him off. Dekman delighted in doing just that, then sitting back to watch the show. Which always made Peter feel a bit bad.

Maybe Preacher Sal had some mixed-up ideas about things,

like the way the government was monitoring everybody, taking fingerprints and such and storing them in a super-computer. Dekman loved to tease the preacher about that, provoking him with outright lies. "I hear they're putting surveillance cameras in all the alleyways now, Sal. You heard about that yet?" and "That old shopping cart you drag everywhere, you think the store isn't tracking that buggy? There's satellites up there watching everywhere you go!" and "I'd love to give you some money, Sal. Really. But then you'd have to answer to the Men in Black!"

Peter changed his mind about Preacher Sal after Sal called him over, sat him down, and asked him, if he was so smart, to explain all the markings on paper money. All the symbols and wavy lines and extra colored threads and reflective strips and dots and dashes. Peter had never looked at a bill before, *really* looked. As an artist, he had to admit that there was way more detail than was strictly necessary. He had to concede that the ways of the government were mysterious and the bills themselves were stranger than most people noticed.

After that Preacher Sal had taken a special shine to Peter and even introduced him to the workings of his personal faith, which were mostly too bizarre for Peter to understand, especially with the weird way Sal talked, like he'd made up his mind to use every word in the English language at least once, it just didn't matter in what order. After an hour of Sal's merry-go-round way of talking, Peter was more confused than when he started. He was happy just to accept that in Sal's world, Sal was a preacher, and the preaching he did was his own business. Well, his own business and the business of anyone remotely in earshot.

But spending time with Sal right now wouldn't get his stomach filled. And he did have Dekman's twenty bucks. So Peter just waved as he passed Sal on his way to the inevitable: the mall. Mulling over Preacher Sal's strange beliefs, Peter piled a table with food — beef burritos and chicken burritos from Taco Time in memory of Anne, double New York Fries, and Orange Julius — and stuffed his face for the first time in weeks. The gluttony felt so good, all the worries he'd been carrying around just faded away. He even considered calling Ellen again. He got as far as standing up to head over to the bank of phones — *Look, our slave arrives with more shiny sustenance!* — when the sound of something, something barely audible, forced him to stop. It was a buzz, a low electronic hum.

It sounded weirdly familiar.

Peter sank into a seat by the Bagel Bin. *Concentrate!* There was noise everywhere, the logjam of sounds familiar to anyone who has ever spent serious time in a food fair: chatter, couples squealing into separate cellphones across a table from each other, the burble of a fountain recycling some toxic soup from the underground parking lot up into the eating area where everyone could enjoy it. Muzak flowed underneath it all to keep the kids on edge.

No. Peter turned his head, straining to catch it again. No. Then he heard it. Yes. There. It was there. A processed tingle like the sound electric fences make in cartoons. A dangerous noise. An exciting noise.

Peter struggled to shut out the distractions all around. He closed his eyes and focused, remembering again the dreams he'd been having, the whiteness of light, the whiteness of sound. This was different, more in its intensity than anything. He couldn't describe it, other than to think that it was like the dream-sound maxed out, cranked to ten. He concentrated on shutting out the yells and footsteps and cash registers. The noises joined into one sound, flattened out, digitized into a whir of power. Soon, it was easy to focus on it: there was nothing else.

Peter opened his eyes a crack. The mall was gone. Everything was gone. Everything but the whiteness and the noise, pulsing from his feet up through his head.

"Whoa!" he said. "Am I dreaming?" Was he talking out loud? He tried to remember the tests to tell if you're awake. Can you dream about wondering if you're awake? Peter was fairly sure you could. He pinched himself, which hurt but didn't seem to change anything. Could he be dead? Does pinching hurt when you're dead, if you do it to yourself? Obviously it didn't hurt if someone else pinched your corpse, but what if you pinched yourself in, like, limbo or wherever this was? Could he really be dead? OD'd on cheap Mexican food and petting-zoo stink and car exhaust? Was that possible? Peter screwed his eyes shut, willing it all to end, and felt a surge of anger: This wasn't fair! He was too young to die. People had said that at his father's funeral: "Such a good man, such a waste, he was too young, taken before his time ..." Peter wondered what a better time would have been.

Hey, maybe his dad was here! He opened his eyes again and looked around. Nothing. He rubbed them, blinked one open, one shut, switched to the reverse. Still nothing. He snapped his fingers, shouted, did jumping jacks.

Zip. Could this be the afterlife? It had never occurred to Peter that life after death could actually be more boring than life itself.

Figures.

He glanced down at his body, which had faded into the same whiteness of his dream. That did it. Hearing whooshing electric noises and seeing white haze was one thing, but losing your own body was serious. He took a deep breath — *remember, Peter, patience and concentration* — and assessed his options, which basically came down to two: either he really was dead or he'd merely gone insane.

Okay, three: he'd been teleported to an alternate universe. Out of those three, he couldn't begin to say which one was the most attractive.

"Hello!" Peter yelled. "Anybody there?"

He winced. Lame. Staring into the nothingness around him, he felt a flicker of fear.

"Yo!" he yelled again. "Hey!" There was no echo, no reply, nothing. His voice was absorbed so that not a drop of sound remained. He tried to run, but without any passing features to indicate his movements, and without a body, without wind or light or shadows, how could he be sure he was moving at all?

Fear deepened into panic. "Okay, the novelty has definitely worn off. I'm seriously finished here. Hello? How do you turn this off?" He sucked in a big breath and screamed — first a little yelp, stupidly afraid to make a scene, then again with all his strength. Nothing. There was no way out of this nightmare, no sign of the food fair, no door marked NORMAL: THIS WAY. He tried to remember his dreams. He'd always managed to pull out of them, but they'd never been this intense. What was the trick to stopping this dream-vision? How do you wake up when you're not actually asleep?

"Abracadabra!" he yelled. "Hocus-pocus! Open sesame!"

Still nothing. He tried to calm himself down, to think. He remembered drama class: *Breathe, breathe down into your belly. Again.* He remembered his father: *Reduce the possibilities until only one solution remains.*

"Shazam! Tur-r-r-rn OFF! Reboot!"

Peter had to face facts. He was no longer at the food fair. He was no longer in the world at all. His pathetic, uneventful, too short life, the only life he would ever know, was over. He was alone, surrounded by white. No, not surrounded. He *was* white. He and this ... stuff were all part of the same nothingness. He tried to connect these statements into some meaningful answer. He started eliminating possibilities at warp speed. The heaven thing was just too weird. Maybe it really was an alien abduction? Get real. Drugged by the taco place? Mmm ... nah. What would be the point of wasting drugs on someone who didn't have any money? Mary-Beth was always warning him about the perils of missing breakfast. Was it a low-carb coma? But he'd just had a major pork-out. Carb overdose? An allergy? Epilepsy? Maybe he had some disease nobody knew about. Maybe it had been there all his life, just waiting for this moment to kill him. But wouldn't he know? No! Because he was adopted! That must be it: he was having a congenital breakdown of the brain.

Panic won. Peter heard whimpering and realized it was coming from his own mouth. He took in another lungful of air and screamed "HELP!" Nothing.

If I just get out of here ... Peter paused. What could he offer up as a bargain? What would be meaningful enough to allow him to escape? Should he promise to go home, make up with Ellen, be a better son?

Yeah, right.

He screamed again and an image appeared in his mind. His voice was a knife cutting through the haze around him. He yelled again, focusing straight ahead and presto! — a slit appeared, a few feet of three-dimensional colour hovering in front of his eyes. It was the most disorienting thing. There was the mall, there were his table and his tray, like a single bar of a movie playing on an otherwise blank screen. He poured everything into widening that slit, into pushing on the imaginary knife he'd dreamt into being, and, trembling, he squeezed through and back into his own body.

Loud! It was so loud! And bright! The lights glared and strobed around him. If this was what getting high was like, no thanks! He felt nauseous and looked down to shield his eyes from the glare and catch his breath. In front of him sat his same old smoothie, thick and room-temperature now. *How much time had passed?* All day he'd prayed for the hours to speed by to get his panhandling over with, and now that

he finally had somewhere soft to park his butt, the minutes
— hours? — had just vanished.

Oh-oh. Speaking of vanishing, Peter spotted mall security approaching, a kid who could barely be out of high
school himself but was insanely tall, probably six foot six,
and gangly. He had sideburns so bushy it was hard to see
his ears. He looked like a baby Ent from *Lord of the Rings*.
The kiddie cop bent way down and asked, "Are you all
right? You've been staring at that cup for quite a while." He
studied Peter for a long moment, took a sniff, then added,
"Are you on drugs or something?"

"What?" Peter asked. "No. I'm … fine. Thanks. Really."

The guard paused, then shrugged and headed back into
the crowd. As far as Peter could tell, no one else seemed
freaked by his little whiteout. Oh God, he was having
whiteouts. Can you die from whiteouts? What was happening to him? Mary-Beth would know what to do. He'd have
to screw up his courage and call her.

But Peter didn't call Mary-Beth. He justified it because
he had no idea what time it was back home. The last thing
he wanted was to get a just-woken-up Mrs. Kennedy on
the phone sounding sorry for him. *I'll IM her tomorrow,*

he promised himself. *There must be an Internet café around here someplace. Dekman won't notice a few bucks gone.*

His conscience satisfied, he treated himself to an orgy of games at a nearby arcade. Twice he tensed, thinking he heard that unnatural hum again beneath the bleeps and the bangs. But each time it passed. *You're fine*, he told himself. *It's no big deal.*

He checked his watch again. The LED was already missing a few of the little bars that made up the numbers so it was impossible to tell what time it actually was. "Cheap piece of crap," he muttered. By the wall clock he saw that it was 8:45 and ducked out of the arcade, chucking the timepiece on his way out. He headed cautiously through the downtown streets, stopping to watch a DJ in the window of the Nike store mixing songs — it sounded like a mashup of the Road Runner theme song and Iron Maiden's "The Reincarnation of Benjamin Breeg" — back to the McDonald's where he had first met Thumper and Spike and Cat. For once, he didn't feel a burning McNeed. He watched for cops, and stopped to listen to a filth-covered bag man preaching hellfire and damnation but left before the guy noticed him.

Peter wondered once again about this group that treated Dekman like their king. Cat and Thumper and Spike, of course, but there were others too. Each day, as he sat panning, kids came by to say hi. They were different ages,

but except for a few eccentrics like Cat, they all wore the
uniform of the street: jeans, hoodies, elaborate jackets, Doc
Martens, all black, plus chains and spikes and piercings.
As he headed to the library bathroom two blocks over, Peter
would see them playing hacky sack on the sidewalk or hanging out by the movie theatres with their dogs. A few of them
tried their luck with the squeegee at red lights. A lot sat
hunched in doorways stitching flags and badges onto their
jackets, a beautiful art form Peter had never noticed before.

Peter had also begun to notice another art: intricate tattoos
that swirled and bled across their arms and legs and necks
and bellies. Scraps of these images would flash when someone stretched to snag a hacky sack or wipe a windshield and
they were the most intricate and surprising things Peter had
ever seen. Dragons. Thorns. Fire. A devil. A burning eye.

There was something else Peter noticed. Marked or not,
jeans or camo (there was even a guy who seemed to wear a
different skirt every day), they all had one thing in common: when they talked about Dekman, there was respect
in their voice.

Stroke of nine and there was Dekman outside the fast-food
place. He was wearing a long dark coat, a watchman's cap

and sunglasses. He looked like a white Blade.

"Peter," Dekman nodded as he approached. It was impossible to see his eyes. "When we first met, I was rash. I presumed. I was wrong. You have shown yourself to be reliable, faithful. A new life awaits you if you want it. But first, I have three questions. Will you answer truthfully?"

Peter thought this whole goth thing was a little corny but also undeniably cool. He tried to spot another person anywhere in sight, but the streets in all directions were deserted. There were only him and Dekman in their little pool of street lamp yellow. Dekman's voice was so quiet and serious. Peter decided to go along. "I will," he answered.

Dekman nodded again. "Good. Peter: do you find yourself alone in this world, forsaken by family and friends, your former life behind you?"

Peter had never said much about himself, except that he'd run away from home. It was creepy the way Dekman seemed to understand him, but maybe it wasn't that hard to guess. His story was probably the same as a million others.

Careful not to betray himself, he said simply, "Yes."

Dekman seemed satisfied.

"Peter: do you accept me and mine as your new friends, your new family, your new life?"

Peter hesitated. Did he? A new family? That felt like the

last thing he needed. If anything, he had too many families already. His own. The other one he hadn't even begun to understand yet, out there somewhere but without him, without the baby they must have just left in some hospital for someone else to worry about. Who could do that to a defenceless baby? Who could turn their backs on their very own child?

And friends. Was he really finished with his old life, his old school, all the kids there and from the neighbourhood? Mary-Beth? Alternate readings in English? Art? The little attic that he was already beginning to forget? He tried to imagine climbing back onto the coach and reverting to the old Peter, dropping back into his life the way he'd dropped back into his body after that terrifying vision at the mall. It seemed unlikely, as unlikely as his father returning from the dead. Some trips are one-way. Some decisions are non-refundable. This was a fresh start. A simple choice.

"Yes."

Again Dekman seemed pleased. Peter noticed a faint scar that curved out from under his sunglasses down to the corner of his mouth. The night air was so cold their breath hung in the air between them like smoke. The blackness around their circle of light was absolute.

"Peter: do you freely and willingly accept the rules and traditions of the tribe, and renounce your former name as you have your former life?"

Things were moving too fast. He knew he should be cautious, each question seemed to demand a higher price than the last, but the time for caution had passed. He was tired of being careful. He was tired of being lonely. It was a night to be reckless.

"Yes."

Dekman pulled off his sunglasses and gave the ghost of a smile. "Then welcome. Now, I have something to show you."

It was a monstrous house from another era, three storeys and so wide it seemed more like a train station that someone had pulled apart, shuffled, and tried to put back together. With limited success. A sheet of paper was stapled into the wooden front door. It was the only clear spot on the door; the rest was covered in layers of graffiti, some so old it looked like it had come with the house. But the words on the paper were completely legible: LEGAL NOTICE, NOT SAFE TO OCCUPY. NO PERSON SHALL REVERSE, ALTER, DEFACE, COVER, REMOVE OR IN ANY WAY TAMPER WITH THE NOTICE UNLESS AUTHORIZED BY and then the rest of the sentence was obliterated by deep red Gothic script: DEKMAN.

In all the time Peter was to spend there, he never did figure out how many people actually lived in the house. They changed with the seasons, sometimes even from day to day. The rooms themselves seemed to change too. A kitchen one day would have a bathtub in it the next. There were storage closets that became bedrooms that became living rooms that became rooms he was not allowed to enter. Sometimes he was sure windows had walled themselves up. Doorways became dumbwaiters. It haunted him. He could feel its presence in his dreams. Sometimes he thought he could smell it on his clothes, sweating from his pores.

The night of the initiation, though, the house was just a dark hulk at the end of a long deserted street at the edge of a city on the far side of the country. It literally was the end: the road terminated at the front door.

As the house came into sight, Dekman's cell rang. Peter could hear its muffled buzz from somewhere inside the folds of the coat, but the older boy ignored it and raised his chin toward the building.

"Welcome. This is the squat. This is your new home."

He let out a piercing whistle and heads popped out of windows all along the building's front. "Dekman's back!" Peter heard an echo pass through the building as the call was carried deeper, from upstairs to down and into the basement, until the front door burst open and dozens of kids hurtled out and down the path to sweep them up in a mad swirl of shouting and laughing.

"Fresh meat!"

"Party!"

After that, Peter's memories got a little scattered. Hands high-fiving him, slapping him on the back, handing him endless bottles of beer. A parade of kids in black introducing themselves, each name more outlandish than the last. Motley. Wrath. Kali.

The next impression was a long and winding march to the beach, blocks and blocks of empty lots and boarded-up buildings. The whole way, kids breaking off and racing into the darkness, then reappearing like dive bombers or bats. At the beach itself, Cat walking across the sand on her hands. Music so loud it was like weather, so loud he could feel it and smell it and taste it sliding down his throat, some freaky deep house beats Peter had never heard before crossed with Skinny Puppy industrial noise. Booming drums. Feedback. Screaming.

At some point, Dekman reappeared. He'd lost the sunglasses and painted a thick black smear of something that looked like uncooked clay around his eyes, which pulsed out from this mask like searchlights set on overdrive. It was so unnerving Peter had to laugh. Dekman yelled something at him that got lost in the chaos, then pointed toward the surf.

Peter followed him to the towering bonfire blazing beside the sea. Dozens of kids danced around it, splashing into the water, kicking sand. Flames glinted off sea and sweat. The music was even louder now. It almost knocked him off his feet.

Peter laughed again. The whole night was insane.

"The time has come to make good on your promise." Dekman's voice was soft beside his ear. Close. Almost inside his brain.

"Shut your eyes. Concentrate. Choose your name."

Peter closed his eyes and tried to block out the madness around him. In the dark, he recalled the mall and its waking dream. He tensed, afraid that he might hear the buzz again. The roar around him faded. *Was that it? Was that the hum?* He sent his mind speeding away from the present moment.

He concentrated on the running itself, on going faster and faster. Faster than any human being had ever run. He knew his body had not really budged, but the hum faded and as it receded, he thought of all the other things he was running from: his father's death, the mystery of his birth, the limits from his mother. Hunger. Fear.

When he opened his eyes Dekman was looking intently into his face.

"Well?" he asked.

Peter leaned closer and whispered into the tall boy's ear.

Together the two approached the surf. Someone killed the music. The only sound on the dark night's air was the crackle of wood and the hiss of sparks kissing waves.

"Tonight we bring another into our tribe," Dekman called. "Willingly and freely has he turned away from his former life. Willingly and freely he asks to join us. Do we welcome him?"

Up and down the sand, kids yelled and jumped. "YES!"

"Then," Dekman shouted to Peter, kneeling beside the surf, "come and be anointed."

Peter approached the water and Dekman scooped up a handful, which he sprinkled on Peter's head. Then he stood and turned back to land. Raising his voice, he yelled, "From this night on, there is no Peter. There is only ... Runner."

"Runner! Runner! Runner!" the kids chanted.

Suddenly, Dekman grabbed him and whispered, "You will never speak of the squat or what you see there. You will never leave until you are allowed to leave. To remind you of this covenant, you will be given the mark of the tribe." Spike broke from the crowd, holding a long branch he'd pulled from the fire. Its tip glowed in the darkness.

"No!" Peter struggled to free himself. "Help!" Nobody moved and there was no escape from Dekman's grip. The pain was the last memory he had of the last night of his old life.

THREE TO GET READY

CHAPTER NINE

Runner hung up the pay phone — *Thank you, slave* — and turned to find Cat standing ten feet behind him.

"What?" he asked. He'd been caught and he knew it.

"Who ya calling?" All around them, the city ground along, oblivious to them and their little drama. He'd chosen an out-of-the-way spot next to the five-storey parkade all the government workers used. At night, it was a bitching skate park. But during the day, it was under constant supervision and surveillance, so the kids kept away from it. At least, he'd hoped.

"Nobody," Runner answered.

"That was five minutes on the phone with nobody, then,"

Cat said, narrowing her eyes as she studied his face. "Phoning home?"

Runner hesitated. Dekman discouraged the kids from talking about their past, but there was no actual rule against it, or against calling your mother for a long-distance fight, as long as you didn't let it interfere with your revenue. That was Dekman's only actual rule: keep making money. Oh, and don't tell anybody anything. Runner still had the pain of a hole burned into his leg to help remind him of that.

Cat was more open than a lot of the kids. Over a few different breaks, he'd heard a bit of her story. She actually brought it up, without him even hinting or anything. She was an orphan. Her parents died in an apartment fire when she was twelve, and she'd been sent to live with a foster family.

"It wasn't bad," she'd said. "It wasn't, like, Baudelaire orphans or anything." Runner knew the *Series of Unfortunate Events* books and smiled.

"But," Cat had continued, "it wasn't great, either. They were nice enough. They'd had their own kid, but he died. Heart attack. Eight years old and he died. I guess it happens."

The next time they talked, it was like no time had passed. Cat just picked up where she'd stopped before.

"Trouble was, the guy worked at the prison. He was, like, a social worker or something. Not a warden, but he spent time with the cons every day and he brought his work home with him. Or at least, the attitude. I swear, I might as well have *been* in prison, the way he acted. There were rules for everything. Too many rules to remember, and I just couldn't catch a break. There was so much punishment, I don't think even he could keep track of it all. Half the time, I don't think either one of us knew why he was giving me another beating."

"Why didn't you run away?" Runner'd asked.

"Run away? Well, I did. A few times, but I had Thumper to think of."

Runner just stared. "Our Thumper? Thumper with the hair?"

"Yeah, what did you think? Of course our Thumper. He's my brother."

"What? You and Thumper? You're brother and sister?"

"Yeah. Why is that so hard to believe? He's a total JD, I know …" JD. Juvenile delinquent. The kids on the street used it like a compliment. Runner willed himself not to remember how his father used to use the same term. Different life. Different person.

No matter how much time he spent with these kids, it was like opening a secret box only to find another secret box inside. And another inside that. Endlessly. You'd think Thumper and Cat being brother and sister would have come up by now. Runner didn't know what to say.

Cat shook her head. "Anyway, it got so bad I'd have to believe in reincarnation just to fit in all the years of punishment that I was supposed to get. And for nothing. Little stuff. Nothing."

"I'm sorry," Runner began.

Cat interrupted. "It's ancient history. Don't worry about it. Finally, Thumper and me skipped out one Sunday while they were at church." The two came downtown and Cat had taken a job under the table at a fish market in Chinatown. That's where Dekman first noticed her.

"But your folks—"

"I said it was nothing."

Now Runner guiltily pocketed the last of the change he'd had out for the pay phone, without answering Cat, and the two of them set off back toward the main drag. It was almost noon. Pedestrians and motorists yelled and slammed on their brakes as Cat and Runner darted back to the public library, which was one of Dekman's many offices. Outside the building, Cat suddenly seized Runner's sleeve and pointed up into the sky.

"See that?"

"See what?"

"That jet, it's … oh, it's just gone behind a cloud. Wait. There!"

Runner peered into the blue and caught sight of a plane breaking from a cloud, a white track trailing behind it.

"Yeah. I see it."

"I heard those things drop, like, chemicals and stuff."

"What? No they don't. That white streak's just part of flying."

Cat gave him a pitying look. "Uh-huh."

When he kept staring, she gestured at the smudge blurring in the wind. "How can you be so sure? Ever heard of chemtrails? Dekman told me about them. The government doesn't allow any commercial aircraft to leave emissions over populated areas, but somehow they're allowed to junk up the sky any way they want. Why? Because the government has some plan that we don't know about."

"So, what? The government is dropping poison onto its people? Is that what you think? Like, mind-controlling substances? Mood manipulators that keep all the workers docile or something?" Runner paused then, and looked at the sheep in suits grazing on the sidewalk all around them. A student bent over beneath the hugest backpack Runner had ever seen was holding the library door open for them.

Runner squinted at Cat. "We're late." Even though he felt stupid for doing it, he held his breath until he was safely inside the building.

As they crashed up the stairs, heading to the third floor,

Runner thought about his visions. Maybe it was *chemtrails* that were making him zone like that. Maybe the government *was* somehow poisoning his mind. But why him? What special threat could he possibly pose to the government?

Nah. That was just too *X-Files*.

"Runner! Hurry up!"

On the mezzanine level, he caught sight of a special display in the children's section. It was mounted on a table and above it hung a Bristol board sign: SELF-ESTEEM. There were swirly flowers and rays of light coming off the letters, which was lame, but it wasn't the artistry that attracted Runner. It was the material itself.

Over the past few months, cardboard had practically disappeared from the city. There was a bonanza after Christmas, which the squat celebrated with a party so big and so loud Runner wondered if his hearing would ever go back to normal. But then the new year hit and supplies dried up. His morning scrounge for sign-making supplies was becoming ridiculous and Runner was frustrated. He'd actually taken to casing art stores, thinking he might have to pull a Thumper and try to jam a two-foot sheet down his pants when no one was looking. But here, in the middle of the children's section of the library, was — he appraised the sign — eight square feet of prime pulp, unsupervised, practically begging to be liberated. It was an opportunity not to be missed.

"You go on," he said, digging into his pockets and hand-ing over his morning's take. "I'll meet you outside after."

Cat raised her eyebrows but continued to the third floor and Dekman.

Runner, meanwhile, sauntered over to the display like self-esteem was perhaps the most fascinating concept he'd ever encountered. *Wow! Self-esteem! Why have I never seriously considered the importance of self-esteem before? What a useful display to get a fellow musing on the place of self-esteem in a healthy, like, psychology.* He gave the display the once-over. There was a table, maybe four feet long, with poems and stories and whatever mounted on flag poles and stuck into plasticine. In the middle stood a mirror with a piece of masking tape across the top. Runner bent down and found himself staring into his own face. *Winner* was branded across his forehead.

The shock he felt came from his general appearance. Runner had started panning in mid-November and it was now almost the end of January. Those ten weeks, not to mention the lack of sleep and the fast-food diet, had taken their toll. His face was getting fat and his skin was paler and zittier than he remembered it. His hair had grown in after the self-administered pruning but now it fell in lank waves instead of curls. He looked like a cheap lawn ornament that had been left outside over one too many winters.

The cut above his eyebrow had left a scar, which, along with the brand on his thigh, would be with him until he died. He bared his teeth and growled at his reflection, checking his gums in case he was getting scurvy. He had no idea what the actual symptoms of scurvy were, but he and his dad had watched *Mutiny on the Bounty*, so he knew that bleeding gums were a concern. His gums didn't look so hot. Maybe he should look up scurvy while he was here. Suddenly he remembered he was trying to stay discreet.

Straightening and glancing up at the sign, he checked to make sure the back was blank. Perfect. Peering higher, he saw it had been hung from the ceiling tiles by regular string. It was a simple matter of yanking the string out, slapping the sign against his side, and heading back down the stairs for the exit. Too easy.

Runner had learned many things over the past couple of months, and one was this: if you're going to steal something, act like you already own it. Look before you grab, but once you're carrying don't move your head, don't check what everybody else is doing, and never look up. Whatever happens, there's no problem.

"Excuse me! Young man!"

Runner heard the librarian's voice from the top of the stairs but he forced himself to stay calm. He could see the exit below and the security cop chatting with some woman next to the electronic gate. He listened for more shouts, but she was obviously hustling around the desk to intercept him. If that was her plan, she could bid farewell to her little cardboard treasure. Runner nodded to the rent-a-cop as he made his way through the barrier and out into the street, clutching his booty. *Avast!*

Down the block, Runner bumped into Preacher Sal again. Literally. Runner was looking back over his shoulder to make sure he hadn't been followed when his thigh crashed into something metallic and painful. Preacher Sal and his inevitable shopping cart. Runner started to come up with an excuse to get free of the old man when it occurred to him that if he stuck with the preacher for a bit, he'd be better than invisible. Sal was so attention-getting that everybody around him just kind of faded in comparison. Even cardboard-hoisting library thieves …

Preacher Sal was more than happy to have a captive audience for a few minutes. It gave him a chance to share some of his personal philosophy, and with a sympathetic youth who might not yet see the true nature of reality but who might be encouraged to open his eyes.

As far as Runner could follow, it seemed to boil down to this: Preacher Sal believed that our world was only one world, that an infinite number of parallel universes ran alongside our own, like pages in a giant book, bound together but separate. This was one thread that Runner actually caught. Some of these universes were happy places, lands of bliss that some lucky people stumbled across in their dreams or remembered from before their births. Our understanding of heaven comes from glimpses like these, he would argue. Near-death experiences are actually brief visits to worlds beyond our own, ditto déjà vu. Leaps from one page to the next. Sal had some complicated theory going about time, too, twisted like a pretzel, larger on the outside or something. Runner quickly got lost on that one — and he was more patient than most of the kids, who just rolled their eyes and bugged the preacher to show them what he'd found lately. Nobody scavenged like Preacher Sal.

Sal was holding forth on something — identity? — when Dekman and Cat came up to them on their way out of the library with the morning's earnings. It was the only time Runner ever saw Dekman really lose it in public. Usually, he'd save his more psychotic behaviour for the squat or some deserted parking lot or construction site. But Sal's preaching literally stopped Dekman in his tracks.

There was no love lost between Preacher Sal and Dekman, and maybe that's what made the old man start up on hell. "Unfortunately," he said, addressing Runner but keeping one eye on Dekman the whole time, "there are worlds out there that make our suffering on this Earth seem like a never-ending pleasure fest."

He shook his long scraggly beard. "There are those among us who must be ever-watchful or maybe they will fall off this plane of existence altogether and land in the fiery pits below our sight."

He chanced one direct look at Dekman. "Fiery pits below our sight," he repeated.

"Open your eyes, old man," Dekman yelled, exasperated. "Fiery pits would be an improvement on this place. At least it'd be warm there!"

As always, Sal rose to the bait. "Oh, my darkful doubter. The fiery pits are no final destination. Oh no. There are worse places that beckon."

"Old man, crawl back in your dumpster! You know nothing!"

Preacher Sal rose to his full height, eyes flashing. "I know these drugs of yours disrupt the natural layering of the planes." People were gathering. This was a show even for Sal. Spit flew as he yelled to Dekman. "I know peril lies in wait for those who refuse to accept their place in the Great Book.

And I know the special hell that lies in wait for you."

Sal lowered his voice. Runner inched away, worried about the cardboard booty still under this arm. Dekman violence was entirely possible at this point, and if so, he wanted to be on the other side of town, like, immediately.

"Hell is not other people, not for you." Sal sneered. "There is a page with your name on it, Dekman. A page of one, just for you."

Suddenly he seemed to come back to himself and the audience clustered around. "Hell," he declared, his eyes flashing, "is only a word for suffering beyond your comprehension, heedless hedonists. Beware!"

People drifted away after that, as Sal gathered up his buggyful of stuff and wobbled off down an alley. Runner couldn't bring himself to look Dekman in the eye, but headed back to his corner, mulling over what the preacher had said.

He was tempted to hang the sign over the front door of the squat just the way it was. SELF-ESTEEM would make everybody laugh, but that wasn't why he'd taken it. Runner worked late into the night on his creation, applying layer after layer of colour to the stiff cardboard.

It felt good to be creating again. He often wondered what Mrs. Fraser was teaching in art this year. His drawing skills were getting rusty and he'd never mastered perspective anyway, not that the kids in the squat complained about the more technical aspects of the murals he was slowly covering the walls with. It turned out that panhandling paid the basic rent, but any extras had to be negotiated. Like food. And for one hellish week, permission to use the bathroom — until Runner found a bathroom on the top level of the house that nobody seemed to know about. He paid with murals. One piece seemed to give him about a week's worth of breakfast, dinner and midnight snacks. Lunch time was downtown anyway. He'd started with the front door, which he painted like a close-up tongue, red and wet-looking. He thought it was too Rolling Stones–ish, but nobody else complained. Probably because from a distance it looked like bleeding flesh.

That was his cue for the next painting. Across the main living room wall he did a dragon chomping on a policeman, and the squatters loved it. He drew dialogue balloons and let them write in what the creature and the policeman were saying. What they put was pretty predictable, but he laughed as much as anyone. In the kitchen he did another one of Amazons with breasts so huge they'd never be able to stand up in real life, then three panels of superheroes swooping down to steal candy from babies with death's-head skulls. Slowly his cartoons took over the walls of the squat. He felt like he was drawing out his personal demons, painting all his fears and his fantasies for anyone to see. Pretty soon the whole squat would look like Runner's imagination. Would that be a good thing? He wished he'd never started but the kids bugged him constantly for more. They wanted their portraits next, and they were always giving him gifts of paint that they had "liberated" for him. Sometimes it was house paint. Sometimes it was craft paint. Spray paint. Automotive paint. "Paint's paint," they said, treating him like a fussy customer in a divey restaurant.

Runner had to admit he was lucky. He got to draw, the kids thought it was cool, and it paid for food. He just wished there was more light to work by. The squat's electricity could never be counted on, and the lights went off without warning all the time. Then it was battery time, and it was hard to get the details right without electricity.

There were always candles. The place was full of candles and smoke, most of it from joints. Early on, Dekman had insisted Runner try dope, so he had. *If Frankie Mulholland could see me now*, Runner had thought, sucking in the smoke and remembering that long-ago day at school with Frankie's dad's cigarette. Instantly, he fell into the terrible whiteness, but this time it was different. Unable to concentrate enough to get back out, he felt disoriented and abandoned. It had been a horrible experience, though the rest of the squat thought it was hilarious, him on his back kicking and clawing against the air, eyes shut fiercely against the brightness only he could see. At least now he knew how stupid he could look when he was lost in his head that way.

"A bad trip on just one toke!" they laughed. Still, Runner didn't need a second chance to learn his lesson. He'd gone straight-edge: no drugs, no alcohol. Just to be safe.

Which made him something of a freak at the squat. There were a lot of drugs there, more drugs than food some days, always with Dekman in the middle of them. Parties could start any time, for any reason, but two things set them off without fail: sunset and Dekman.

Runner had quickly learned that his initiation that first night wasn't really different from any other night. The house was constantly full of noise and dancing and skateboarding and the merry destruction that the kids got up to when they were high. Some of it got on his nerves — at least the power outages killed the guitar jams, which could go on for hours — but mostly it was okay. It reminded him he wasn't alone. But the parties had another problem. Parties meant Dekman, and not just Dekman, but the crazy super-Dekman Runner had seen the night he joined the squat.

Dekman without brakes was a scary thing, a force of nature people shouldn't have to live through twice, like hurricanes. Dekman without brakes was capable of absolutely anything, any flavour of psychological torture or physical attack. He transformed from a bossy brainiac control freak into Satan himself with a pocket full of dope and a house full of junior demons at his beck and call. Runner had seen more than one kid run from a party, bleeding or screaming or both, with Dekman laughing like a madman from the porch.

On nights like that, Runner would pack up his stuff and head back downtown. When Dekman asked him later where he'd got to, he'd explain that he had so much paint, he couldn't possibly use it all up at the squat. "I was restless. I had all this paint. So I went and tagged St. Stephen's."

St. Stephen's was the Catholic cathedral on the way to the university. It was maybe ten blocks from where Runner usually hung out, on the other side of downtown from the squat. He liked to go there to get away from the other kids, who never went there because there was nothing to steal and nobody to beg from. Runner felt bad tagging a church, but since the poster paint was actually water-soluble, he figured it wasn't too bad. His work would wash away in the next rain, and it rained almost every day.

"Yeah, I did the skull and crossbones across the door there at the side," Runner boasted.

"Those are the porches of the transept," Dekman replied. You never knew what Dekman was going to say. The lights were off now and Runner, holding a candle up to the finished work to take one last look at the Bristol board, figured he had done enough.

"Sweet," came a voice over his shoulder.

It was Dekman. Of course. Dekman had this spooky habit of sneaking up behind you completely silently. He'd never met anyone who could be so quiet when he wanted to be. And so loud at other times. Dekman was holding a cigarette, which Runner realized was actually a joint when he lit it off Runner's candle. Dekman offered him a hit, but Runner refused with a shudder. Dekman was leaning over Runner's shoulder, exhaling sweet smoke, admiring the drawing, which showed a boy being torn apart by evil-looking birds. The character was standing with his arms stretched out and the birds were flying off with ragged gobs of flesh in their beaks. Bolts of jagged light burst from the wounds.

"Now what would your guidance counsellor have to say about that, young man?" Dekman teased him. Runner wordlessly flipped over the sign and showed Dekman how the two shapes were mirror images, the swirly letters of SELF-ESTEEM following the same outline as the carnage on the reverse. The happy rainbows on the positive side were the streaks in Runner's version.

"Hidden depths!" Dekman said with delight. He blew out more of the skunky smoke (*Ssssssssssssigarette*, Runner remembered), then told Runner to stop hiding in his room and get downstairs. It was clear it wasn't a request.

Runner picked up the candle and paused. Looking down at the vibrant markers spread out around him, he marvelled again at the irony that someone who loved colour so much dreamt only in white. Staring into the candle, he took a deep breath and made up his mind. "Once and for all," he whispered to himself. "Just to know."

He tried to clear his mind, to erase the sounds from around the house. He heard Dekman call from downstairs: "Runner! Get down here!" It was like being at home still.

3 … Kids skated up and down the stairs, howled at the moon, cranked the stereo.

2 … Runner pushed away memories from the day, droids trudging past on their way to their exciting lives herding paper. Kids cruising by, squatting down to read him his horoscope. Silver dropping. Silver not dropping.

1 … He concentrated on the shimmer at the heart of the candle's flame.

The sound and the space came together and Runner opened his eyes to a familiar empty scape. He lifted a hand. Nothing.

Ka-bloom!

The interesting part, what he'd worked so hard not to think about during the long days on the street and the nights of painting and partying and skinny-dipping at the beach and doing mischief around the city, tagging walls with Dekman's Jolly Roger mark, was how to get out again. At the mall, he'd somehow made that doorway. He was sure of that. That had been him. He'd needed to get out and it had happened. Runner was sure the white world, as he now called it, came from inside him. It wasn't an attack by aliens, or some seizure of the brain. It was a power that Runner had. A dream made real somehow, and for some purpose. What that purpose was ... okay, was not clear. But it was a power nonetheless, and powers, he knew, could be harnessed. You only had to read *X-Men* to know that.

That knowledge had come to him lying in bed after his disastrous drug experiment. While the floor vibrated to the rhythm of six electric guitars playing death metal, Runner recalled every moment of that experience. What interested him was how different it was from all the previous trips into that whiteness. Now that he had something to compare it to, he realized that usually he had a feeling of peace. Sure, he'd panicked the first few times, especially that night at the mall, about what might happen if he couldn't find his way back into his usual life. But each time, everything had resolved itself and he'd made it back inside himself with no harm done. Really, there was no cause to worry.

Now, lying in the squat, Runner ran through every experience he'd had. That first time in the parking lot after the fight. Okay, maybe that didn't count. Those waking dreams in the park by the hostel, then again at the beach. The nights dipping into the blankness, then the first hum of power he'd heard at the mall while he waited for Dekman. Every time he'd had the same sense that all his troubles, all his fears and anxieties, were being protected by the hum, separated from him and cushioned. He remembered the sense of a hallway, how comforting that had seemed before he came to fear the loss of control.

Runner put his thoughts into words. "It isn't *like* a corridor. It *is* a corridor. It's a hallway and it's there to guide me somewhere, somewhere safe."

If only he could figure out how.

Cautiously, Runner tried to command the nothingness: "Door."

He looked around. Nothing. Louder: "Door!" Still nothing.

He tried to remember the various words he'd spoken that night at the mall, but even as he was cycling through them he was pretty sure the trick wasn't some special hocus-pocus. He just wasn't trying hard enough.

Runner screwed up his eyes, concentrated all his being on the whiteness in front of him, and suddenly remembered his last coherent thought from the mall. The knife! He pictured the power of his thoughts like a blade. Like a penknife blade jammed into the asphalt of a windswept prairie truck stop.

Feeling the hot anger of injustice and self-pity, the blade of his mind sliced through. Once again a clean sliver of colour hovered before him, revealing a slice of his room at the squat.

He pictured the line swelling into a doorway. As it widened, as more and more of his room appeared, Runner smiled to himself and let out the breath he hadn't even realized he'd been holding. He stood in the whiteness, his room pulsing in living colour in front of him. He turned his mind around. If his room was in front of him, if his troubles were packed on both sides of him, what was behind him? The whiteness seemed to continue into the distance. He squinted to the very edge of his sight and thought that there, just at the edge of what was visible, the whiteness took on a particular shape. Like a handle. Or a knocker. Interesting.

CHAPTER TEN

The next morning, Runner was counting change outside the library, like he always seemed to be. It was getting up to noon on one of those rare winter mornings when the clouds burn off so fast you can watch them shred and disintegrate, like paper on a bonfire. Runner felt a moment of peace. Hey, a coffee sure would be nice right about now. *Dream on*, he lectured himself. *It's accounts time.* For the captain of an army of street kids, Dekman was a stickler for promptness and detail. He had a system and he stuck to it. That's one thing you could say about Dekman. And if he thought you were slacking, if you were late or came up short or couldn't say where you'd spent the morning or even smelled like you'd been hanging out somewhere warm, the trips to the library or the bus station or the mall or the hotel lobbies could be deadly. It was worse than school. It was worse than a visit to the principal's office.

An image of Mr. Patterson leaning across his desk, hair waving like undersea kelp, flitted through Runner's mind, but he squashed it with hardly any effort. Anyway, he was feeling too good to dwell on the past. Dekman was right: focus on the future. Don't worry. Be happy. Or high. And he had every right to be happy. The sign had been a huge success. One guy, a regular who worked at the bookstore down the block and was usually good for a few quarters in the morning, had even offered him cash to take it right then. Runner told him he needed it for the rest of the day, but he'd listen to an offer after five. Like the guy would pay. He was probably just messing around. Anyway, Runner wasn't sure he could sell the picture even if he wanted to. It was the first piece of real art he'd done since the fall. Everything else — the murals at the squat, the Dekman graffiti, the daily signs — had been for a laugh or just to freak out the sheep on their way to the shearing shed. The guy did wear nice clothes, though, and expensive shoes. He'd pay.

There was a trickier problem, though: Runner needed somewhere safe to stash his little money maker while he went up to see Dekman. This wasn't like the usual signs he could just carry with him, or leave with one of the other kids. The cardboard was boosted from the library in the first place. Somebody there would see the other side of it, the SELF-ESTEEM side, and raise holy hell. Dekman was clear about this: nobody got on the library staff's bad side. The place was one of Dekman's favourite spots, smack in the middle of his various territories. He called it the board-room. Runner probably shouldn't have taken the sign in the first place, but Dekman had liked it as much as anyone. "Hidden depths," and all. Still, better not to go looking for trouble. Runner couldn't leave it with one of the other kids, either, since all's fair in love and scavenging, and there wasn't anyone downtown he trusted enough to hold on to it without stealing it or selling it.

There *was* one person who would appreciate it as much as Runner did himself, someone who wouldn't scuff it up or sell it or anything. Preacher Sal.

There was one subject Preacher Sal and Runner definitely agreed on: cardboard. It was Sal who noticed all the cardboard was disappearing from the city. It was one of the hundreds of things he kept in his buggy and he seemed to need fresh supplies on a regular basis. Whether he used them up in religious rituals or for sleeping on, Runner wasn't sure and didn't want to ask, but he was always on the lookout for extra pieces, because if he couldn't use a scrap for one of his signs he would pass it along to Sal. The preacher was even known to trade his other stuff if the cardboard was high-quality. One time he fished out a pair of high-tops that were practically new, only one size too big. Another time, a bag of ketchup chips.

Sal took him once to show him where all his swag came from. Behind the bus station, the two stood on a small hill and looked through the chain-link fence at the surreal landscape below. It was like the gods had picked up a thousand lost-and-found boxes and shook them out over this particular incline. Discarded suitcases. Empty boxes. Ripped clothing. Chipped dishes. Widowed shoes. Two-wheel tricycles. Hollow televisions. Each item so forlorn, so undesirable that Runner had felt himself tearing up at the pointlessness of it all.

"The wages of sin," Sal said, spreading his arms wide to take in the raggle-taggle display. "The detritus of despair."

"But where does it all come from?"

"Thieves and vagabonds. Men of scant honour."

Runner checked to see if Preacher Sal was putting him on. "You mean, guys knock off stuff and then what they don't want they just pitch here? Why here?"

"The ways of man are indeed mysterious."

Threading his way now through the midday throng,

SELF-ESTEEM sign jammed under one arm, Runner thought maybe Sal was on to something after all. Sure, a lot of his ideas were a bit old-school street-crazy for Runner, but one thing made sense: Sal's belief in worlds beyond this one strangely matched Runner's visions. Since the previous night's experience, he'd been back into the white world twice already, once at the squat as the sun rose and once just sitting there on the sidewalk watching the bare branches of a little tree sway in the breeze. Runner felt confident that he was edging closer to being able to control the vision. The more he visited, the easier it became. And less scary. He felt drawn toward that little blip at the periphery of his seeing, sure that it was not a barrier but an entranceway into something. He felt surer, too, of his power to exit the blankness inside his head. It didn't mean he understood the place at all — he didn't — but it gave him a boost of confidence to feel that when he found himself in nowheresville, he could at least get back again.

He was tempted to tell Sal, but something made him hold back. Once the preacher knew, everyone with one working ear would know, and Runner wasn't ready for that level of attention. In fact, he was trying to avoid attention of any kind, willing himself to fade into the colourless cement that was his daytime home, letting his signs speak for him. For now, he would keep his secret inside, try to figure it out by himself. It might help make the days pass faster, he figured, give him something to think about.

I'm special, he tried to convince himself. *This proves it. I won't be panning forever, stuck under Dekman's thumb. I'm never gonna end up like Dekman, or Spike, or any of them.*

"Hey, buddy! Use your eyes!" A passing taxi leaned on the horn as Runner almost wandered into traffic. Snapped out of his reverie, Runner realized he had ten minutes, tops, before Dekman would miss him.

Sal was down by the harbour, scattering bread crumbs to a courtyard crammed with pigeons, lecturing his "flock" on his usual theories about God and the government.

Runner waded into the middle of the sermon, waving.

"Preacher! Hey, Preacher! It's me, Runner!"

Runner had learned it saved time to identify himself to get Sal's attention. The old man sent another spray of crumbs arcing across the cobblestones, employing the same gesture that smiling women in bikinis use to showcase prizes on daytime TV. The pigeons scattered as the food pelted down, then started burbling dementedly as they hoovered up the offering. The sound made Runner think of underwater wind chimes. Preacher Sal smiled with satisfaction.

"Eat of the goodness, children," he called as he crossed toward Runner. He had noticed the sign. The smell of him made Runner's eyes cross.

"Have you brought a supplication, my young disbeliever?" Sal asked.

Runner had no idea what this meant, but then he usually had no idea what Sal meant, so he just barged ahead. "Preacher, I got a favour to ask. Can you hold on to this for me? Just for an hour?" Maybe he'd have time to hit the arcade after he saw Dekman.

Preacher Sal reached for the cardboard and fingered its ply, nodding as he raised it to his beak for a sniff. It must have passed inspection, because he set it on top of his buggy, where it leaned like an iceberg about to calve. He didn't spare the ink on either side the slightest glance. For him, the true nature of the pulp glowed through whatever defaced it. There was nothing like the innocence of board, he would say, the purity.

"Thanks, Preacher. An hour. Max. I just have to go see Dekman —"

Sal jerked to attention, scattering stray crumbs caught in his robes. "That hellion! He will find the fires burn hotter than he imagines. For every flame will burn as three for him and their heat will be a cleansing. Oh yes, there are those who follow the movements of man and see that when the viper swallows the rat the rat does not always cease to be!" He shook his head, then seemed to notice Runner standing agog and bent down to him. Runner was amazed the smell could actually get worse. "But this is not your worry. Yes, for you I will give safe harbour to this paragon of paper, this bounty of board. Though it will tax an old, frail soul such as mine ..."

He paused and licked his lips. This was Runner's cue, and he passed over a Kit Kat for holy consumption.

"One hour. At St. Stephen's," Sal directed, patting the sign affectionately. "And then let us also discuss the scarcity of this one's brethren. I have discovered a most troubling explanation for its orphanhood. The pressed fibres do not remove themselves willingly. We must discuss conflagrations."

"A conflagration is a fire. Don't they teach anything in school these days?" Dekman replied when they settled down to business in the accounting section of the public library. Dekman had been reading *Profits for Dummies* and *How to Make a Million Dollars Without Really Trying*. "Why? Where'd you hear that word? Has someone been talking about fires?"

Runner checked himself. It didn't do to catch Dekman's interest. And there had been something in the old man's face that told him this was more serious than his usual paranoid ramblings. "Nah," he muttered. "It was in *Ninja Night Crawler*. I was playing it at the arcade."

"Video games have come up in the world," Dekman declared. "I don't remember any 'conflagrations' in *Doom*." He brightened at the sight of Runner's take for the morning. "This is fine, Runner, very fine. I knew you had hidden talents."

Runner was sent back out into the street with instructions to report back if he saw three squeegee kids who'd been kicked out of the squat for stealing drugs from Dekman. Rumour had it they were trying to sell them on the street, and Dekman had a very special surprise in mind for them as soon as they were found. Runner hoped to steer as far clear as possible of the whole conflict.

On his way downstairs, Runner met Thumper on his way up and flashed him a smile. "Hey," Thumper grinned back.

"Hey." And with a nod Runner was back down the stairs, past the cop, through the glass doors, and into a cold afternoon on the first of February.

Three months, he thought. *This is three months.*

CHAPTER ELEVEN

The afternoon erupted into a small-scale storm. The clouds had been threatening all morning, but the rain, when it came, was unlike anything Runner had ever seen. Worse, Preacher Sal never showed, and Runner ended up getting into it with some AA guy standing outside St. Stephen's, smoking and nodding up at the deluge from under the awning the two shared.

"She's really coming down, eh?" the guy asked, pointing needlessly up into the sky. Runner was feeling irritable, and shivers were running up and down his body. His clothes were soaked. "You here for the meeting?" As though he could sense the trembling, the guy added, "You gonna be warm enough in them skimpy rags?"

Runner concentrated on ignoring him and tried to call up the peaceful blankness of his imaginary world, but the stink of the cigarette (*ssssssssssssigarette*) kept distracting him. Runner was one of the few kids at the squat who didn't smoke, which was another thing he and Cat had in common. She thought smoking was stupid, that it was just giving in to the mainstream to start puffing away like you were some kind of movie star. Tobacco, anyway. She wasn't nearly so opinionated about pot. For some reason, she was especially relentless with Thumper, who just looked wrong with a butt hanging out of his little choirboy mouth. She'd snatch perfectly good smokes right out from between his lips and throw them into traffic. He always looked both ways before lighting up now, and it wasn't cars he was afraid of. "At least you know what's in a joint," she'd yell right over top of a roomful of people at a party, ignoring all the glares shot in her direction. "Do you have any idea the garbage they put into cigarettes? Tar and asbestos and acids and crap you wouldn't feed your dog and you idiots suck them up like they're the best thing since deep-fried Mars bars!"

Deep-fried Mars bars were a Cat favourite.

Runner made it a point never to lose it with the kids from the squat, where fights happened more or less every day; sometimes Dekman cheered them on, sometimes he kicked the kids out altogether. And on the street,

Runner just ignored whatever the clockwatchers had to say. *Go home. Get a real job. Make something of yourself. Take a shower, why don't you? Don't throw your life away.* But there was something about this AA guy that made Runner snap.

"Stop blowing smoke in my face, would you? And shut up!"

Mr. Nicotine goggled at Runner.

"Hey, man—"

The smoke got into Runner's nose and set off an extended coughing fit.

"I mean, what's the point of quitting one drug if you're going to start up another one that's just as bad?" The fellow, who didn't seem that much older than Runner, opened his mouth, but Runner plowed on, raising his voice over the growing wind. "In fact, it's even worse. At least booze doesn't stink like cigarettes."

Runner's full-on vent, however, was cut short by an attack of wooziness. The guy closed his mouth, no doubt afraid of another verbal attack from a clearly unstable street person, but then he took another drag; in fact, he was defiantly chain-smoking.

"Forget it." Preacher obviously wasn't coming and it would be just like Dekman to send someone to check up on him with the weather so crappy. He was sad about his sign, though. He pushed off, not bothering to look back, and, suddenly dizzy, staggered down the street, trying to dodge the worst of the deluge. He felt so tired he was tempted to lie down right there in the flooding road (*wolves circling* ...). He made do with a soggy shuffle.

Runner was suddenly sick of the panhandling routine, of his whole so-called life. He didn't mind asking for money, because he didn't really ask, his sign did. And he didn't mind sitting outside all day. He was spending more and more time trying to understand the blissful emptiness of his imaginary world of blankness. He felt he was close to figuring out its secrets. And in the meantime, he could just park his body wherever and hope nobody stole his panning bowl while he was out of it. It didn't matter to him what was going on around him while he zoned out, which maybe was more like drugs than Dekman, for one, realized. Anyway, even the longest periods struggling to understand the whiteness seemed to take only a few minutes in the real world. It was hardly time to have his body stolen for medical research or anything. He didn't need to bicycle-lock himself to the pavement or anything. And even when he was concentrating on the street, it wasn't so bad. He liked watching the people walk by. It was more interesting than sitting through math.

What really pissed him off were the trips to the library at lunch and then back to the squat at the end of the day to hand over the money.

It was *his* money, even if Dekman insisted on taking every penny. He'd earned it, hadn't he? Runner figured he must have given up a couple hundred bucks in the past few months, and for what? What had Dekman given him in exchange? Fast food for breakfast, lunch and dinner. Some cupboard at the squat to sleep in. The tribe. And protection. Dekman was always going on about the deals he'd worked out with the police to leave his kids alone, and it was true that Runner had never been hassled, but was that really thanks to Dekman?

At least now he knew how the older boy could afford all the fancy clothes and the cellphone, the cigarettes and drugs. The tribe lived off the nine-to-fivers, and Dekman lived off the tribe. Runner had an idea where all this was heading. They'd done *Oliver Twist* in English, and he remembered Fagin, the ringleader of all the pickpockets. Things had ended badly for Fagin, he seemed to recall. Runner had a feeling that life with Dekman was going to end up badly, with someone in prison or hospital. Or worse.

Still, it was easy to think these thoughts when he was on his own. It was harder to remember them with Dekman there in his face. The older boy's wild ideas and ambitions washed right through Runner, as powerful as the rain slamming down now. Water was strong enough to erode stone, he remembered, and Dekman was the same: he could be so innocent and friendly when you first met him, clear like water, but actually just as cutting, just as corrosive. Just as prone to freezing cold and boiling steam.

The rain was picking up, if that was possible, and Runner started to worry he might drown from breathing in so much water. The ground was cold, the air was cold, the wind was driving all sensation out of his face. People walking by were shouldering their way against it, collars turned up, already looking forward to warm soup and crackling fires at home. Nobody was going to stop for some homeless kid with weird hair and grimy clothes sitting in the middle of a wind tunnel. Wind tunnel. Where had he heard that before? He had a sudden memory of Mary-Beth, blurry in the distance, a red apple held out like a beacon toward him. She hitched up a book bag onto one shoulder, turned and disappeared.

Without his cardboard sign, Runner was reduced to begging out loud. Every word was broken by fits of coughing. The attacks left him feeling wrung-out. Wind snatched at his every breath.

It was just his nerves. They were getting the better of him, that was all. Looking up into the storm, he remembered a scene from *Mary Poppins*, when the kids jump into the drawing on the sidewalk, the one the Dick Van Dyke character, the chimney sweep, does with the sidewalk chalk. That had always been his favourite scene, one he used to play outside his own house when he was still young and drawing with sidewalk chalk seemed daring, *this close* to writing on the walls.

Runner watched sheets of water plummet from the sky, waves of pedestrians pushing through. He looked for Thumper, Cat, anyone from the squat, but the streets were emptying as the storm picked up strength. *Good*, he thought. *Suits me fine. I hope it never stops.*

"I hope it never stops," he said out loud. One thought swelled to a flood.

"... a flood," Runner heard himself say, "and everybody's perfect little life washed away." And louder: "I hope all you robots, you sheep with your Gore-Tex fleece and your cellphones and your stupid Tilley hats and your takeout Frappuccinos, I hope you lose it all. Washed away, like those sidewalk drawings, everything smearing into one big smudge."

Clink. A woman in an elegant camelhair coat dropped a quarter into his empty paper cup like this was some performance she could tip for.

Runner took a ragged breath, sucking up a lungful of mostly water. His breath whistled in his ears, louder now than the traffic. "All your pretty little pastel lives! Erased! And then people like me and Thumper and Cat, we'll be on top! Me and Thumper and Cat. We'll be in charge. See how you like it then, living on the street, living in the crud and the wet and—"

Runner was crying, but he couldn't stop. He was on his feet, he was shouting as the people walked by. All the weeks of fading into the greyness of the city, of avoiding attention and keeping his thoughts to himself, of hiding his loneliness and suffering and loss, all of that was over. He wanted to be seen. He needed to be seen.

"You'll be at the bottom and we'll be on top. Like *Big Brother*. Who's gonna last, eh? Who's gonna last?" he bellowed at a couple of elderly tourists. "You gonna get kicked out next?" Runner yelled at a man walking by with a young child clutched in each hand. Runner blinked his eyes free of tears, watched the kids' ladybug rubber boots splishing past, protecting their innocent feet from the muck and the garbage, the muck and the garbage Runner called home. The girl swiveled her head and tracked Runner as she disappeared behind a curtain of water and wind.

"Or you?" he shouted at a woman talking into a cellphone as she lifted a shopping bag up out of the splash of a passing car.

"Except it's all fixed, isn't it? Who's gonna win. This isn't

Mary Poppins," he told a bus driver blowing on a coffee as he waited for the light to change. Runner was feeling dizzy now. Everything was blurry with tears and rain. He could barely see as far as his feet. He felt hot. His croaky yelling couldn't compete with the mash of traffic. More convulsive coughing. He couldn't remember what his point had been, wasn't sure anymore why he was yelling, felt each breath bring less oxygen into his body. He really was drowning in this rainstorm, an idle thought become prediction. Somehow he was drowning in front of all these people. Where had all these people come from?

Mary Poppins. That was it. "The penguin waiters, the carousel horses. It's somewhere to go. Don't you see that?" he asked a bike courier. Runner swayed against the wind, his breath a knife wound. "It's some way to escape the chimneys, the dirt." He realized the man who'd given him a shoulder to lean on was a policeman. He tried to push off, but his body had other ideas. Strong arms held him up. His father used to hold him this way when he was little. Jack would lie on the bed and hold Runner above him, arms and legs stretched out, a starfish swimming through air. In the doorway, his mother would fret over spinal injuries and other roughhouse accidents.

His father's arms were so comfortable, so strong. Runner felt relief just to be held. He'd missed his dad, missed him so much. There was something he had to tell him, something crucial. But it was drowned out by the growing buzz. Where was this buzz coming from?

"Oh, no. Not now," he whispered, fighting for focus. "Not now."

A glare, a gauze of white. Then nothing.

CHAPTER TWELVE

Runner was painting. He was painting meadows and flowers and trees. He was painting petals and grass blades and leaves and streaks of cloud and nuggets of fresh, soft earth. He worked slowly, savouring the details. He paused often to try to recall the specifics, to get the details just right, but he couldn't exactly be called a nature expert. However, sometimes we're not even aware of the information we're taking in as we pass our days. Osmosis. Like Sal's paper money, with all that extra *stuff* beyond what's actually needed: a five, a ten, a fifty. The painting was going well, given how big it was: larger than his usual stuff. In fact, life-size.

Runner had discovered the purpose behind the whiteness.

He'd finally figured out its meaning. It was a corridor that held back the terrible facts that can be part of life, yes. An enormous and welcome security blanket he could wrap himself in against pain and sorrow. But it was more too. It was a passageway leading away from the real world altogether. Runner had finally straightened his shoulders, turned his back on reality — being adopted, being father-less, living in the squat — and headed into the whiteness, all the way to the horizon. And there he'd found the handle that had always seemed to beckon to him. With his new-found confidence and excitement, it was easy for Runner to grab hold and tear aside the whiteness. The handle gave way. The nothingness gave way. It was the easiest thing in the world, once he believed he could do it. And behind the nothingness, he found — something different.

Something Runner was painting into life.

It started with a thought, as change so often does. A stray thought flitted across Runner's brain and changed his life in one intuitive flash. He just felt sick of the whiteness. That was it. The thought came to him: *I'm sick of all this white. I wish it had some colour.* And in front of his eyes, the whiteness split like pure light in a prism. Runner thought of that stupid Pink Floyd album his dad had loved so much, with the single thread of light hitting the triangle and turning into a rainbow. No matter how many times his dad explained it, Runner always thought it looked like a gay-liberation picture. Which was fine, but not, according to Jack, what the band had in mind back in the day.

Here, it was easy to split the whiteness in exactly the same way, pulling every colour in the crayon box out of the void. And even cooler, Runner could send those colours back again by folding them back up into the whiteness. It was like watercolours: smears of red, blue, green that bled into each other and could be washed over if he wanted to erase and start over. In fact, he liked erasing and starting over. And it didn't matter if he did. It wasn't like he had to go out and buy more paint if he ran out. He had an infinite supply of materials. He was pretty sure that none of this was real anyway. Maybe he'd died or the world had ended, though that didn't really explain all the times he'd nearly made it this far. He remembered Sal's belief of worlds within worlds. That was too complicated. Maybe he was just insane. That was possible. In fact, not such a big deal. He was grateful that there was nobody to tell him what to do, nobody to push him out into the damp to beg for change, nobody to send him long-distance clichés. *You've made your bed and now you'll have to lie on it.*

He got tired of watercolours. They were never his favourite medium. He preferred something a little more vibrant. He was still discovering the rules of this place.

(It turns out there are rules everywhere, even in places that seem to have no rule keepers.) In this place, Runner could only try things and see if they worked. If they did, he figured he was following rules. If they didn't, he was breaking them. Willing colours into being worked. Blinking whole landscapes to life didn't. So Runner willed. Soon, he managed to blink small things into being and out again, which was a lot easier but didn't really suit his role as creator. Not enough drama. Now, he'd wave his arms wildly back and forth, like he was doing tae-bo, and things would literally streak in and out of existence. Or mistakes would go away. Sometimes, if he felt frustrated, he'd hurl lightning bolts at some second-rate smudge and watch it burst into flames. Or shrink it smaller and smaller until it disappeared with an audible pop.

Overall, as he swept his eyes across his creation, he was pleased. Everything was turning out all right. He'd decided to build a landscape based on shows he liked, historical ones like *Lord of the Rings* and *Xena: Warrior Princess*. He wanted the calm country peace you get on shows like that, at least the calm before all the roundhouse punches and kung fu kicks. He'd started with the sky, tinting it a vivid blue, almost the shade of a tropical sea. He was leaving a wide band of nothing along the horizon until he decided what to do with the edges. That was something else he remembered without knowing he even knew it, all those hours in art learning how to rough in the horizon for composition and leave the details for later.

He'd settled on a short-leaf grass for ground cover. He'd taken it from his memories of *Madden* NFL. He'd started with a small island of green at his feet, a perfect circle of grass bordered in all directions by more nothingness. The sight made him think of his mother's golf course, and he burst out laughing. Now *this* would be one sight that would leave even Ellen speechless.

He was starting to enjoy crazydeadland.

Runner closed his eyes and took a deep breath. He held his arms out straight, fingers pointed, and began to spin. As his hands whipped around, he imagined the grass flowing from his fingertips, rippling across the ground. When he opened his eyes, he was disappointed. Green extended as far as he could see, but it looked fake, like a gym covered in Astroturf.

He thought back to Mrs. Fraser's art class. What was missing? He tried to see the landscape around him in two dimensions, like a picture. It came to him. Perspective! That was it! It looked fake because it had no depth. He hurled features — hillocks, trees, meadows, boulders, anything that came to mind — in every direction. Big ones up close, small ones farther away. He paid special attention to angles and shadows.

Good! This was good! This was better than good! But it all just ... sat there. Nothing moved. There was no sound.

It was soothing after months sitting in the middle of down-town, but kinda boring too. It should be more like a video game, more interactive. What happened when he moved? Would he just drag the same landscape around with him like an astronaut in a bubble helmet? Curious, he started walking and was pleased to see that the objects were behaving themselves, staying put, growing and shrinking logically. He dropped to the ground and sniffed the grass. It smelled good. It looked good too, up close.

Worn out, Runner leaned against a stone elephant he'd stuck on top of a little hill and took a breather.

Ah, peace. He closed his eyes and dropped a brilliantly red rock, as large as a skyscraper and shaped like a devil's head, down beside him. Head tilted back, Runner yelled up at it: "You're not bad. You're just drawn that way!"

There was a lot missing. Wildlife, for instance. He'd managed moving water, and even a breeze, which he was proud of, though so far it just coasted at one speed like a sedan on cruise control, not pausing to take in the surroundings or get to know the natives. Still, a breeze was cool. *Ha, a cool breeze!*

Tentatively, he tried his hand — his mind, really — at a squirrel. Except he wasn't sure what a squirrel looked like. Rats with bushy tails, he figured, so he focused on that. When he was satisfied with what he'd made, which he worried looked more like a gopher in a wig, he yelled

"Go play!" It scurried off, in search of some friends, no doubt. Runner felt bad for the little rodent, so he made another. This time, he breathed life into it. Literally. He took a deep breath and pictured a rainbow gust swirling, enveloping the squirrel, animating it and sending it out to frolic.

He was pleased. Now the two squirrels had each other. He hoped he'd made a boy squirrel and a girl squirrel. He didn't want to spend eternity cranking out new squirrels. Maybe he should invent a squirrel photocopier next.

Runner wondered how much time had passed since he'd entered this place. In the whiteness it had usually been only moments. Assuming there still was a real world out there somewhere, with his body stuck in it, were the minutes passing slowly? Or had his mind crossed into another dimension entirely? Maybe years were rushing by while time hung in this land, like a solid bank beside a racing stream. Had Runner stepped outside time altogether or was he buried in a single instant? Was he on the shore or in the stream? Either way, was he still himself, still growing older, still inside his body? Or had he split into pieces, travelling through time at different speeds? Would he ever return to normal life?

Did he want to?

One thing was sure. He felt free. In fact, it was the first time he'd felt free since his father died. He remembered the safety he'd found with Dekman and the squat — enough food (even if it was crap), company (kind of), a roof. But this was different. He remembered Spike saying, "I'm a free contractor." Obviously not true. He remembered Dekman at the initiation: "Willingly and freely has he turned away from his former life. Willingly and freely he asks to join us." None of that had been true. Not really. *This* was willing. *This* was free and true. Runner held that freedom and that truth close to him, a precious and fragile warmth.

As Runner worked (he was fine-tuning a field of blue-bells that rang like telephones), he paused to watch his two squirrels gambol past. Were they the same two? They seemed just as happy as he was. Should he do more for them? What did squirrels eat? He felt he should give them something nice, a treat. In cartoons, they were always storing nuts, so he threw some juicy nut bushes down by the river. They were *chipmunks* in the cartoons, he realized, not squirrels, but then maybe what he'd made were chipmunks too. You could take details too far.

He felt lonely. His squirrels seemed so happy together. A crazy thought rose up. Could he do people? Maybe he could duplicate a Thumper. Thumper would love this place. And Cat. And Mary-Beth. It could become like a clubhouse for people he liked. Well, not the real people. They probably couldn't be teleported inside his brain. But his memories of them. If he could make up squirrels without having ever really seen one, he should be good on Mary-Beth. He'd spent hours studying her when she wasn't looking. If he was going to start on people, there'd have to be a guest list, though. No Dekmans allowed. No Ellens. No Mr. Pattersons or Alex Carltons or Spikes or beat cops. No. He'd left that world behind. Both those worlds. People in his face, people telling him what to do, who to be. He was better off alone. The squirrels would keep him company.

His face broke into a smile. People or no people, there was one lost thing he could recover. He lifted one wrist and wrapped the fingers and thumb of his other hand around it. He squeezed tight, feeling skin on skin. When he took his hand away, there it was: Mary-Beth's friendship bracelet.

That was a good start.

His mind swung up into the sky and wheeled around to look back down. He saw his own body stretched out beside the water. Talk about out-of-body experiences. This place was trippy, all right. He remembered Dekman advertising his dope, promising all the kids that life would be brighter, funner, weirder. It was like living in an infomercial some days, being at the squat. Dekman even had sales sometimes, happy hours, discount days. But this. This would blow Dekman's mind. Runner had a more intense vision going on here than Dekman could ever hope for. Straight-edge.

Runner looked down on himself and was pleased to see a smile on his own face.

What this place needed was a name. Something magical, something new. With a name it would seem more real, more like somewhere he could imagine living in. The more he looked around, the more clear it seemed there wasn't much that was worth going back for. He had everything he needed right here. And if he didn't, he could desire it into being. Maybe this was heaven. Maybe he'd been right all along.

He dropped back into his body — flying was tiring — and turned down the volume on the stream he'd created. He could redraw it farther away, but that seemed like too much work. He rolled over and dropped his head in for a drink. Was this water real? Was it quenching a real thirst? It sure was cold. And wet. He plunged his whole head in, then shook it dry. He caught a watery glimpse of himself in the surface of the stream. Kneeling there on the bank, Runner concentrated on his reflection and tried to figure out what was real and what was not. Was there any difference between, say, this stream and his own body? Between the water and the air? Because if not, then this body of his, the one he'd been carrying around his whole life, was just like the grass and the squirrels. Temporary. Changeable. He took a breath, stood, and lifted his arms, cupping his hands like a corny comic-book magician. "Up!" he boomed. Nothing happened, and he felt a twinge of disappointment. Then he looked down. The ground was eight feet away. Runner beamed. "All right!"

Buoyed by his impressive new height, he blinked a Twinkie into his hand and took a bite. For an instant, it tasted the way he imagined clouds must taste, but then the chewy sweetness kicked in, so that was fine. Chewing, he looked all around. It was still a world in progress.

Runner had a sudden inspiration. With great solemnity, he called out to all the tinkling flowers, to the stream, to the ringing bluebells: "I name this world … Runnerland!" Another image rose before him, the glint of bodies by firelight, the searing pain of fire on flesh.

Runner cast it aside and returned to his normal size to check on his little squirrel friends. Suddenly, he heard something that made him pause. It sounded like his name, like someone was whispering his name. He turned his head this way and that, tracking the sound, and realized, too late, what it was: a call back to reality, a call he didn't want to answer. He tried to stay with the creamy snack, with the breeze and bluebells, but the noise was stuck in his head, was pulling him, his whole world, back into white. Runnerland faded. Going. Going. Gone.

Runner opened his eyes and saw Cat standing over him, in what seemed to be a hospital room. She looked so much like one of those relatives in corny movies fretting beside the bed that he burst out laughing. Her eyes flashed in anger, but then she laughed herself. She dropped onto the bed beside him and started testing how high the springs could bounce her. He felt like his bones would shatter.

Runner put out his hand to stop her and saw something wrapped around his wrist. Mary-Beth's bracelet! He hadn't imagined it after all! But a second look told him it was nothing more than one of those hospital admissions tags. Runnerland was make-believe after all.

"You look like crap, by the way." Cat said this like it was the best news in ages. "You were so sick," she continued. "You could barely breathe. You had pneumonia. And …" She bounded down to the end of his bed and peered at the hanging clipboard. "And pleural effusion," she read aloud. "I came to see you and this doctor started basically yelling at me and telling me how sick you were. He tried to get next of kin out of me. They'd been through all your clothes, looking for clues, I guess. So then they started on me." She closed her eyes and rubbed them vigorously like she was trying to start a fire.

"As if I would know anything. They told me that if you were allergic to drugs and they didn't know, you could die. Like it was my fault somehow! *I* didn't make you sick!"

Silence. Then Cat whispered, looking into Runner's eyes: "You've been here for two whole days. Do you realize that?"

She began nervously bouncing one foot on the floor, then the other, craning her neck to check on the patients in the other beds on the ward. Runner struggled to reassure her before the bouncing could start up again. His mouth felt dry and his voice was creaky, out of practice.

"Cat. It's okay. I'm okay. Really. I'm glad you're here, though."

Runner felt shy talking so intimately to this strange wild girl.

"But how did you know I was here?" His ribs ached. He reached his arm up to rub his chest and discovered tubes disappearing into his arm. He felt woozy.

"Dekman found out. He knows people who work here. I think that's how he gets those pills he's always handing around. But I never told them anything," she added excitedly. "What would I tell them anyway? I don't even know your real name. Or where you're from."

Runner started to speak, but she held up her hand.

"But if I did know, I would have told them. Runner, they said you could die. I didn't want you to die. I'm sorry."

She took a moment to compose herself, then continued in a quieter voice. "When I told the doctor I didn't know anything, he was really mad. He said he was going to alert services for when you woke up. Runner, we need to get you out of here."

While he got dressed, they plotted ways to sneak him out of hospital — Runner thought maybe Preacher Sal could smuggle him out in the shopping cart — but in the end he just walked out. Stealing away is like any sort of stealing: just pick it up and act like you own it. As Runner tried to walk tall down the corridors, he cradled his chest, which felt like a month-old jack-o'-lantern: firm on the surface, soft inside. Rotten.

"The prodigal son," Dekman said as Runner shuffled up the path and into the squat that evening. "Welcome back. I was starting to think you'd decided not to return. I was starting to wonder if maybe I'd made a mistake with you."

"Dekman!" Cat protested. "He was in hospital!"

"Don't overreact, it's just pneumonia. No big deal." Turning to Runner: "You just need some antibiotics. I know somebody who can get us some. You'll be fine in no time."

Runner tried to look grateful but even smiling hurt, so he just stumbled upstairs and tried to land somewhere soft.

The following Sunday, Runner discovered he owed Dekman a lot of money. They were sitting out on the roof, peering down at a group of kids playing croquet with beer bottles instead of balls, listening to the tinkle and smash of happy destruction.

"Runner. My man. Thing is, you haven't left the house in a week. That's a week of antibiotics, a week of food. It adds up. You see that, right?"

Runner nodded, but said nothing. He was concentrating on the texture of the tree that spread beside the roof. He realized the Runnerland trees needed work on their shadows, especially in the indentations in the bark.

"You're back on the street tomorrow, Runner. Even whole-sale, those meds are adding up. We'll have to move you, though, or you'll get picked up and I won't get my lovely money. Get your rest now." Dekman smirked at Runner's face, then howled as one of the kids below started going berserk with his mallet, playing Whac-a-Mole with a full case of beer. "Save some for me!" he yelled and ducked back inside.

Runner looked up at the moon, just a sliver hooking the lip of the horizon, and it hit him.

"I'm not going back out there, Dekman, not for you or anyone. I'm not going back out into the rain and the garbage and the stupid sheep. I've got a better idea."

There on a mild dim-lit February night, sprawled on the squat's canting roof, Runner closed his eyes, tuned out the voices yowling below and the other ones inside — Dekman, his mother, even Mr. Patterson — and listened instead for the hum of freedom.

FOUR TO GO

CHAPTER THIRTEEN

But Runner did go back to the street. Different corner,
same routine, the cardboard for each day's sign coming
out of Preacher Sal's buggy now that Runner was too
weak to scrounge the alleys and haggle for the good stuff.
Sal seemed to feel he owed Runner something, which
maybe explained where the SELF-ESTEEM sign had gone.
At least he had one friend. Since his time in hospital,
the kids had become wary of him, like they weren't sure
what secrets he might have given up, whose side he was
really on.

A hallucination. Or a dream. Dekman leaning over his mattress. The room is black. Runner has read this line in stories: *Nothing but the whites of their eyes.* Now he knows what it means. Dekman's eyes gleam, gather the fragments of light and reflect them back, like a cat. Not Cat, though. There's nothing gentle or friendly in the look Dekman gives him. Dekman radiates hostility, hatred.

"Dekman. Man. What's up?"

"Runner. You think you fool me. You think you fool everyone. You fool nobody."

"Dekman. I—"

"Shut up. I'm watching you, Runner. I see what you're doing. You sit there on the street. I watch you. You sit there with this little smile on your face, totally out of it. You're having a lot of fun out there on the sidewalk while you're supposedly working for me. What have you found, Runner? Huh? What are you taking? Where are you getting it? Kids are noticing. They're asking. They're saying maybe you've got something better. And that won't do. Won't do at all. This is my squat. These are my kids. Not yours. Mine. Back off, Runner, or I'll give you a reason to run."

Then darkness. Did it really happen?

Runner woke up feeling stronger, almost like before he'd met Dekman and Cat and the rest, like before his dad had died. He remembered what it was like to start the day fresh as a T-shirt straight out of the dryer, clean and dry and warm. The antibiotics were doing their job. Or maybe it was the increasing mastery he felt over Runnerland.

Still, the days disappeared like drops from a fistful of water. Each boring morning, each deadly afternoon Runner took his handfuls of coin to the library or the squat. Dekman was hardly around anymore and Runner would hand his money over to Spike, whose complexion had worsened over the winter.

"It's the light," he said one day, noticing the direction of Runner's eyes. "My skin needs sunlight, and we haven't had a clear day since the damn dinosaurs died. It sucks for my skin and the skating is totally heinous too. I hate this town."

Runner just nodded.

Spike never offered an explanation as to where Dekman was, and Runner never asked. Maybe he didn't know. Still, he seemed as uneasy as Runner about the frequent disappearances. And when Dekman *was* around, he looked tired all the time, distracted. Runner figured he'd been sampling the product more than usual. That's the thing with infomercials: they can't always be entirely trusted. There was a certain buyer-beware thing that maybe Dekman wasn't paying as much attention to as he should. *Contents and finish may differ from those pictured.*

Sometimes Dekman would take one of the squatters off for some private plotting, playing favourites every other day, it seemed. Runner thought they looked more nervous than usual as they went off for these one-on-ones. But the few times he got up the energy to go snoop, they were up to the same old destructive time-wasting activities that always went on.

A few times they'd defaced his murals. Big deal. Runner didn't care. Since that day he'd come back from hospital, especially since the you-owe-me talk Dekman gave him out on the roof, Runner had lost whatever connection he'd felt to the tribe. He could count on one hand the kids he felt any loyalty to: Cat, Thumper, a few of the quiet ones like Twitch and Frenchie who squeegeed down by the highway where Spike and the rest couldn't be bothered.

The more cut-off Dekman became, the more out of control the rest of the kids were. The nightly parties were getting wilder, and there were fires now when the rain stopped, or even sometimes in the rain, gasoline sucked and stolen from parked cars poured on stacks of wood sheltered under the yard's few remaining trees, sparks snapping and sizzling in the downpour. Deranged, savage music feeding their fury. It was surreal, a sight that the Runner of a few months ago would have tried to capture in paint. Now he just turned away. Old news.

As the pay phone receiver rang in his ear, Runner checked the streets again. Not that he cared if he got caught, but life was easier if he was cautious. His hand was full of quarters — two or three minutes' worth, he guessed.

"Hello?"

One word enough to suck the breath out of his throat. Mary-Beth.

"Hello? Is anyone there?"

"Mary-Beth. It's me …"

"*Peter!* Is that really you?"

"Yeah. It's me. Listen —"

"Peter! Where are you? Your mom is in total panic mode. She keeps calling here, like I know where you are. She's been over. She keeps talking to my parents. It's creepy! And everybody at school keeps asking what's going on, where you are. Even the police came to talk to me. Are you okay? Where are you?"

Despite everything, Runner had to laugh. Same old Mary-Beth. "I'm fine. Everything's fine. I mean, it's not, but it is.

I can't really explain. I just couldn't stay. After Dad died, things changed, I guess. I just couldn't."

There was an electronic stutter, and Runner plugged the machine with more quarters.

"Peter, that's long distance. Where are you?"

"—"

"Peter? Can you hear me? Are you *really* okay? Please tell me."

"It's hard to say. There's too much to tell. But, yeah, basically I'm okay. I am. I lost your bracelet, though. Actually, I've lost a lot of things."

"Peter—"

"Mary-Beth. Listen to me."

More stutters and Runner dropped in the last of the coins.

"I can't come home. I can't go back to school. I can't just walk back into my old life. I don't think it's even there anymore. Not after everything. Where I've been. What I've seen. Done. Everything's different now. But I think about you all the time, you know—"

Time was running out. "There's a place I've found, and some day I'd like you to see it. I don't know how, but I'd really like that. It's so beautiful, Mary-Beth. Just like a storybook. It's peaceful and beautiful and nothing bad ever happens there." Words failed him. Maybe he could send her a picture. That would maybe get it across.

Out of the corner of his eye, he saw some tourist looking pointedly at his watch.

"Mary-Beth, I have to go. I'll try to call again soon. If you see my mom, tell her not to worry. I have things under control."

He couldn't trust his voice anymore. He felt close to tears. He cradled the receiver and ended the connection. Runner leaned back against the phone, ignoring the guy waiting and clearing his throat. Runner stared into the distance, then wiped his eyes. Mary-Beth's voice echoed inside his head and his heart.

Fixing his eyes on the city before him, Runner squared his shoulders. A line from English came back to him unexpectedly. *Once more unto the breach, dear friends.* He stooped to pick up his sign, checked the slot for quarters, and headed back to work.

How wrong he'd been. Bad things could happen in Runnerland.

Runner was aware of the change even before he opened his eyes. The forest, usually quiet, was alive with sounds of alarm: hoots from owls ripped from their daytime sleep, cries of eagles and hawks and other raptors riding the winds, growls from the larger animals sniffing the wind. Even the insects chirred with agitation.

Runner listened to the ruckus, realizing that once these creatures of his were set in motion they had their own lives to live. This filled him with a moment of anxiety. He'd been so blithe about bringing them into being. He'd never stopped to consider whether they *wanted* to live here. What had he done? Was he no better than his mother, bossing these things around? Or Dekman, forcing the kids to live by his rules, for his amusement? But his worries were cut short when he saw the horizon. There, between the rise of two mountains, spiking from the brow of the land, he saw it. A plume of white-grey smoke threading into the sky.

Smoke? In Runnerland? Runner rubbed his eyes, closed them, and counted to five. He looked again. There was no mistaking it. A line of smoke hung in the sky, like a crack in a mirror. What could it mean? Had he been careless? Had he wished smoke and now he couldn't remember? Maybe he'd left something burning? He tried to recall if he'd even introduced fire into Runnerland. He didn't think so, although a memory nagged at him, something to do with fire that he'd told himself might become important. Whatever the thought had originally been, it was lost now. But his attention often strayed, especially if he was still caught up in life at the squat, some stupid territorial thing or comment from someone. He knew he ought to treat his special creation more carefully than that. *Daydreams can lead in unexpected directions.* Had that message been a horoscope or a dream?

Either way, he was sure he hadn't been thinking about fire or lightning or anything else that would explain the smoke. This had nothing to do with him.

Somehow, he wasn't alone. He could feel it.

An arm reached across his field of vision, and Runner flinched. He barely had time to take in his surroundings, dirty sidewalk, parade of legs, idling cars, before the hand made contact with his shoulder and started shaking him to attention.

Cat.

She'd broken the trance, brought him back to reality. Part of him felt relief to be free of Runnerland's worrying intruder. But the line of smoke hung in his mind's eye, troubling him. He wasn't meant to be back in the real world right now. He felt sure of that. Cat had interfered, reached across the line in his mind between here and there. It couldn't be good.

"Cat," he said, trying to clear his head. "What is it? What's wrong?"

"Runner," she said, jiggling on her toes and snapping

her fingers as she bounced beside him. She didn't show the slightest sign that he'd been zoned out, though it must have been obvious his mind was elsewhere. She seemed to have more nervous energy than usual, if that was possible, and it seemed to Runner like she was going to explode if she didn't put that energy into something.

He waited but she just kept shooting looks up and down the busy street, scanning the crowds of late-afternoon shoppers wandering by. Abruptly, she started walking an imaginary tightrope on the sidewalk, swaying and catching herself at the last second.

"Cat," he called up to her. "What is it? What's going on?"

Cat shook her head, pigtails slapping her cheeks as they caromed around her small skull. "Where is the little twerp? How much clearer could I have been?" Then, her eyes fixed on Runner although she kept talking to herself. "Let's just head over there. I told him to meet us there if anything happened. He'll figure it out."

"What about my sign?" Runner asked, pointing down at the day's appeal: WILL WORK FOR DOUGHNUTS. "I can't just leave it here. Besides, Dekman gets pissed if I —"

"Forget Dekman. C'mon. Leave your stupid sign there. You don't need it."

"It's not a stupid sign." But she was already halfway across the street, stomping on the yellow divider line and throwing him looks over her shoulder. He shrugged, scooped up the change, and followed. What else could he do?

The route they followed took them around the outskirts of downtown. They were in a fancy neighbourhood Runner had never seen, keeping to a jog. After fifteen minutes, Runner felt like his lungs were going to ignite. Breathing was harder since the pneumonia, in spite of the medicine.

"Cat," he wheezed. "Cat. Slow down." His chest was throbbing, and he was afraid of another collapse. His head was starting to hurt as well.

"Cat! Stop. Tell me why we're running!"

There was a roaring in his ears. Cat was going full-out now, zigzagging across spacious lawns, dodging cars and bikes, racing little yapping dogs to the corner. She glanced back.

"Runner! Hurry up!"

She jogged back. "Runner, you've got to go faster. Thumper told me last night. Spike and Dekman were talking and he walked in. They never saw him. At the house. They were packing, and they were planning how to leave the squat. They were talking about how it was time to clear out. Time to move on, start over."

Runner stared. What would the house be without Dekman? He was the heart of the place — the evil heart, but the heart anyway — and Runner couldn't imagine how the kids would manage without him. Even with Dekman there to keep everyone more or less in line, the chaos was pretty huge. Without him … Well, it would be real chaos. Dangerous chaos.

"Did Thumper ask him what he was doing?"

Cat rolled her eyes. "Have you *seen* Dekman lately? You don't ask Dekman questions, Runner. No, Thumper didn't ask him. But he did see Spike later. Thumper says he asked Spike what was going on and Spike was very nervous. Told him to mind his own business. That's when I told Thumper we needed to double-check on the house. He said he overheard something about five o'clock." She checked her watch. "It's almost five now. Hurry up!"

Runner set off after her rapidly disappearing back. He had a sharp pain in his chest, and breathing was less than pleasant. Sweat ran into his eyes. No matter how often he blinked it away, a mist filled his vision. He swiped at his forehead and saw —

Trees. Runner stopped in his tracks as he almost stumbled into a full-grown evergreen tree of some kind. He was in Runnerland, no transition, he was just there. Without thinking, he raised his eyes to the line where land met sky.

There, straight ahead, the plume of smoke, thicker now, a rope where once there was a thread. Runner stopped to scoop a handful of water from a pool at the base of a tree and found himself kneeling on someone's lawn.

"Hey, kid," a guy called. He must have been eighty, wearing a yellow golf shirt and brown dress pants, watering a gnarled bush at the side of the property. "You get off my lawn! This is my property! You tell that girl too! Go on, git!"

Runner backed off the grass and started up the sidewalk again. Cat was a speck, oscillating at the rise of the next hill. Runner recognized his surroundings now. They weren't as far from home as he'd thought. Cat had brought them in a loose circle around downtown so they approached the squat from the back, from the beach side. They could have walked it in ten minutes as the crow flies, but instead they'd run for twenty. Was she trying to kill him?

As Runner squinted to make out Cat on the hill, his heart began to hammer. Cat was a pulsing star against the smudgy sky, a star dangling at the bottom of a line of grey.

Smoke. Runnerland.

Runner rubbed his face again. The smoke had widened into a cord fraying at its edges, tiny filaments snapping and spreading across Runnerland's sky. The wind had picked up and was teasing out the smoke, smudging a section of sky as wide as Runner's finger.

If the wind is scattering the smoke, he thought, *it could be spreading the fire as well.*

Runner summoned rain. Heavy clouds sprang out of the default midafternoon sky, wicking across and wiping out the usual puffy cumulus. Slow, thick drops parachuted down, flattening the grass blades as they landed. It was like a rainfall out of some music video. A cartoon shower of happy fat raindrops.

"No! RAIN!"

Runner lifted his arms and flapped his fingers, and the lazy pancakes of water shattered and spread into tiny biting droplets, needles to puncture the flames Runner could now glimpse at the end of his vision. He remembered the storm that had sent him to hospital and struggled to recreate it now.

"Runner! Hurry up!"

Runner seemed to have stopped in the middle of a quiet suburban street. Twisting around, he saw he was lucky he hadn't been hit, standing there like a village idiot. Cat was streaking back down the hill toward him, waving her arms and yelling. And behind her: smoke. Real smoke.

"For God's sake, Runner. RUN!"

Ignoring the creak and the pain in his chest, Runner flailed up the slope, meeting Cat halfway.

"What is it?" he forced over the ache. "What's going on?"

"It's the squat. Come on!"

Runner and Cat set off again, cresting the hill and surveying the destruction below. The grand old house was on fire. Top to bottom. The walls were alive with what looked from a distance like dancing paint. Flame rolled out the windows on the top levels and even from a block away the pair could hear the hollow *Woomph!* as roomfuls of fire spread through walls and doubled and doubled again.

Cat grabbed Runner's arm as they watched the first fingers of fire poke through the roof.

"What are we going to do?"

Runner closed his eyes to block out the destruction of what now passed for his home, but the rushing sound remained. He couldn't escape it, even with the covering hiss of rain. Without looking he knew where he was. Runnerland was burning, one snaking line of trees already lost, the stumps blackening the pall of grey overhead. Runner focused on where the fire burned brightest, lifted his arms, and waved them frantically in front of his body.

"Erase!" he yelled. "Stop! Undo!"

It was no use. He felt as helpless as that first time at the mall, trying to control the whiteness with shazams and abracadabras. Helpless to save the squat. Helpless to stop the fires of Runnerland. Raising his eyes, he saw the reason. His forest was drenched in rain, but where the fire burned, the sky was cloudless. It had never occurred to him before, but Runnerland had some kind of edge. Where the flames licked his land, the rain flowed. But his creative powers seemed to stop just short of the house. He summoned a tidal wave to crash across this border, to soak the intruding flames. But the huge wave struck an invisible wall and collapsed back onto all his beautiful trees and meadows, all now turned to sludgy grey. The fire burned on.

Sirens interrupted, spoiling the woodland hush. Cat was pulling on his sleeve. "Runner! Cops! Let's go!"

She was yelling against a wind that seemed to rise straight out of the conflagration. *Conflagration*, Runner remembered, *a fancy word for fire*. Where had he heard that before?

"C'mon Runner. We can't stay here. We've got to go."

At that moment, the roof around the squat's chimney gave way and bricks rained into the house's fiery centre. Sparks streamed from the windows along the front, and the tree in the back yard began to smoke and steam. Pumper trucks pulled into the yard and a crew set to work, trying to save a house that was clearly determined to die.

CHAPTER FOURTEEN

As Runner and Cat stared in horror at the destruction of the only home they had, Thumper wheezed into view. His cheeks were red and he was puffing. Cat glanced at her brother, then gave a double-take.

"You smell like smoke! Thumper, were you down at the house?"

"No. Um. I was having a smoke with some of the guys at the arcade and I lost track of time. I knew you were waiting. I ran all the way."

"You have no idea how worried I was!"

Runner watched the two siblings. It was now so clear to him that they were related, he wondered how he'd ever missed that fact. He marvelled at their similarities. He ached to have someone in the world who looked like him, acted like him.

The wail of an approaching pumper truck snapped him out of his reverie.

"Cat. Thumper. We've got to get out of here. After the fire's out, they're going to start looking for people. If the cops don't find us, Dekman will."

The three took off, heading to the petting zoo where Runner had spent his first nights in the city. It felt very full-circle to him: homeless again, with no shelter but his hidden cave.

"Can we just think this through one more time?" Runner asked, stretching his legs out to catch the last of the weak spring sun. He was hungry and his chest throbbed. This whole living-on-the-streets lifestyle hadn't been the best for his fitness level. He grabbed a handful of twigs and fiddled with them as he talked.

"Like, for example," he said with a grunt as he tamped a piece of wood down into the park's hard-packed soil. "It could be just an accident. The place was a dump and it caught fire. Like, off a cigarette or something. Off a joint," he said pointedly at Cat and Thumper. "Or someone was pouring gas all over stuff out back again. What's the big deal?"

Cat had been picking the heads off snowdrops and now hucked them rapid fire across the grass. "No, Runner. I already said—"

"Cat," Runner interrupted. "I'm just trying to understand here. Let's at least think about some different ideas before we make up our minds." He tried to catch Thumper's eye, but the boy was silent. He seemed much younger since the three of them had turned their back on the squat and hightailed it. Cat flopped onto her stomach and did a few pushups, levering her arms off the spreading roots of a tree. She grunted along in rhythm. Up. Grunt. Down. Grunt. It made Runner tired just watching her.

"God, Runner. You sound like such a sheep. There's no time for that. We've got to figure out what we're going to do. Like, right now."

"Uh-uh," Runner said, stubbornly wedging his butt further into the dip of ground he was sitting in. "I'm not even standing up until I know everything you know. I'm sick of not knowing what's going on. Or else I know one thing, you know something else, Thumper knows something else. Don't you see? That's how Dekman keeps us all guessing. Either I'm in or I'm out."

What did she mean "sheep"?

Cat was standing on her hands now, feet and legs leaning way over one way, then the other, her hoodie scrunched down toward the ground, baring a flash of midriff. Runner looked away, over to Thumper, who was eyeing the pair of them from behind his bangs. Cat finally stopped, upside down, against the tree. She drew in a dramatic deep breath and snorted it back out. "Okay. Fine. Different ideas. An accident. As you say."

"Thank you. One: accident." Runner pointed to the twig rising up out of the ground, then jammed a second one next to it. "Two: revenge. Someone didn't like us, or didn't like one of us, or didn't like the squat, or the drugs, or the parties. So they torched it. Like, neighbours. In fact, I wouldn't blame them. When you think about it, we kind of sucked as neighbours."

Thumper spoke up. "It wasn't neighbours. I already told you. Last night. Spike and Dekman had a plan. They said five o'clock. It was no accident."

"Like I said. We think of all the different possibilities, then we decide what we're going to do." Runner picked up another twig, willing away a memory of smoke hanging in the sky above Runnerland. It couldn't be a coincidence, two fires in his two homes. It just couldn't be. "What else?"

Cat made a face, beat a tattoo into the ground, eyed Runner. "Let's see," her voice dripping sarcasm. "What can we blame the fire on? Volcanic eruption in the basement? Ball lightning? Satanic possession? This is stupid. Either it was an accident or it wasn't. If it's an accident, we hook up with Dekman and figure out where we're going to sleep tonight. If it wasn't an accident, we gotta ask ourselves: who set it?"

"Okay," Runner said, holding up the third twig. "Three: Dekman. Dekman and Spike set the fire." He felt nervous even putting the thought into words. He glanced around to make sure nobody was within earshot, then planted his twig next to the pair in front of him. Not that he didn't have the right to say whatever he wanted, but this was treason. This was *Mutiny on the Bounty* talk.

"Either way," Thumper was saying, "I say we stay as far away from Dekman as we can. All the usual places. And kids who'd rat to him. And we get the hell out of this park, find somewhere safer till we're sure."

"We could just stay here," Runner said, flicking a thumb at the leafy cave.

Thumper shook his head. "Who do you think found the cave to start with?"

Cat's watch beeped six o'clock. She jumped up, raised a Doc Marten over Runner's twigs, and stamped. "Thumper's right. Don't be a wuss. Let's go."

Runner sighed. He looked at Cat's foot, at the broken sticks, at his friends. Something was nagging at him, some point he'd overlooked, some detail that was actually important here, but he couldn't put his finger on it, and he wasn't too hot on the idea of sitting around on his own until he figured it out. Not if Dekman knew the park as well as Thumper said. Not if Dekman was in on the fire. Not if Dekman had finally jumped off the deep end. Runner rose and headed out of the park's shadows in pursuit of the disappearing pair.

And found himself back in Runnerland, watching smoke. Thick, oily smoke spreading across the sky, casting a midnight slick into the heavens. It was malignant, evil smoke. Smoke that wished nobody any good.

From the ridge where Runner stood, he could see the smoke swallowing the last of the blue. He still couldn't put out the fire. He'd tried everything he could think of, but nothing made a difference. Exhausted, defeated, he surrendered. Anyway, the fire seemed to be burning itself out, though the smoke remained.

As he observed, white birds lifted off like sleek paper airplanes at the edge of his sight and threw themselves into the darkness. They capered and loop-the-looped in a display of aeronautical prowess. Runner concentrated on their frenzied flight.

Thick white strokes billowed behind them, contrails like chalk lines dividing the slate sky. They were travelling at superhuman speed — if Runner were back in his normal life he would have called it supersonic, but here? Were they flying faster than the speed of sound? Can living creatures do that? Surely not for real, but in Runnerland? Did sound even have one speed here? They must be machines. Runner had never created anything mechanical; he felt somehow that this wasn't the place for machines.

He stared in wonder. The lines had taken on the outlines of letters … of words … a sentence: CROSS THE LINE.

Runner's breath froze with fear. His mind couldn't accept this.

Runnerland flashed to black.

Cat was waiting with Thumper at the edge of the park. She just rolled her eyes as Runner hurried toward her.

"Finally."

She led them away from the park, careful to avoid downtown or any of the places they normally hung out. They weren't sure who they could trust, so they weren't planning on trusting anyone. They passed some hours in a laundromat and hit the superstore, where Thumper stocked up on supplies for the three of them. Once the stores all closed, they hit the road again.

Looping through streets full of interchangeable bungalows, Cat guided them confidently through a maze of more streets he'd never seen. Every one of them was named after a tree, which seemed totally random to Runner. He realized how little of the city he'd explored in the months since he'd arrived. Cat seemed to know exactly where she was going, frequently breaking into a jog, but then slowing down again. Runner's chest couldn't handle the pace. She finally showed mercy at the corner of Pine and Larch and called a break. Glancing around, she pointed to an alley off Larch. It was so overgrown it looked more like a tunnel than a city lane.

"Down there. We can take a break back there. In the tree fort."

"How do you know all this?" The question hung in the air as Cat studied his face.

"Not yet," she replied. "Let's get safe first." She and Thumper disappeared around the shrubby corner. Runner followed them. He didn't have a lot of choice.

Sure enough, an old wooden fort hung off a tree at the end of a yard halfway down the alley. Grabbing one thick branch after another, Cat monkeyed her way up and into the little house. She didn't even stop to see if anyone was watching.

Thumper followed, even more quickly, and after only a moment's hesitation, so did Runner.

Inside, there was an empty room wide enough to lie down in but too low to stand up straight. There were two windows, one looking back out onto the alley, the other at the silent house. The sulfur light cast by the street lamps down the block was bright enough for Runner to pick out the outlines of Thumper and Cat where they rested against the solid far wall. Their expressions were inscrutable.

"Where are we?" Runner asked.

"Shhhh!" Cat whispered. "Talk quiet."

"What is this place? Cat?" he repeated. "How did you know it was here?"

"We grew up here," Cat answered, and for a moment Runner imagined Cat literally boxed into the fort, sharpening her claws against the walls. He stifled a nervous giggle.

"This used to be our fort. God, we practically lived out here, especially when our parents fought, which was, like, constantly."

"You grew up here?"

"Sure, me and Thumper. We moved here when I was two. Thumper wasn't even born yet."

"This is the foster family! The prison warden!"

"Um, I lied."

"You lied?"

"Well, yeah … There wasn't any foster family. We had a pretty average childhood."

"But the … the apartment fire! The Baudelaire orphans!"

"Geez, Runner. I lied, okay. None of that happened."

"The Chinese fish store," he finished weakly. He shifted his weight and a loud creak in the floor made the three of them freeze.

"Ssh!" Cat hissed. Silence hung heavy for a minute, two minutes. Runner could hear Cat's breathing as they waited.

Finally, she spoke again, her voice soft, hesitant. "Do you have brothers and sisters, Runner? Parents?"

"Cat," Thumper said the name like a warning. He half-turned to peer out through the window.

"Relax, Thumper. It's okay. Runner's right. No more secrets."

Runner took a deep breath and gave the highlights. His dad. The money. The adoption papers. Mary-Beth. Everything. Except Runnerland. He wasn't ready to talk about that yet.

When he finished, Cat let out a low whistle, which Thumper silenced with a fierce shush.

"It's Dekman. He's coming into the alley!"

The three friends ducked below the window.

Runner strained to hear any movement below the tree fort, but there was nothing, not even a crunch of gravel in the lane.

Dekman was either threading his way along the verge of grass behind the houses or Thumper had imagined him. Wait. There. The lightest scuffing of stones in the alley. He was being careful and quiet. There had to be a reason for him to be so quiet, and Runner didn't like to think what that reason might be.

"Does he know about the fort?" Runner asked Cat and Thumper as quietly as he could.

Cat shook her head. "He knows we grew up somewhere around here, but I don't think he knows which house. He's just hoping to stumble onto something. If we wait, he'll give up."

"Dekman never gives up," Thumper said. "I saw him cut down a tree with a pocket knife once."

All three imagined Dekman's eyes running across the boards of the tree house. Any second, Runner was sure, that grin would rise over the window sill like a demonic Cheshire Cat's. Bright moonlight swept into the fort as the wind scoured the night sky clean of clouds.

"Is there any other way out?" Runner asked, getting his first good look around.

"Uh-uh," Cat said, shaking her head. "Just the windows. From there, you're in the alley or …"

"Or what?" Runner asked, inching closer.

There was a moment's pause. "Or into the house. Okay.

I've got a plan. Thumper, do you have anything hard you could throw? Like a rock or something?"

Thumper fished around in his pockets. "A rock? No. Quarters, string, my knife, some gum, my lighter …"

Cat gave him a look. Lighters and fire were not welcome at the moment.

"What about you, Runner?"

Runner swallowed, checked as quietly as he could manage. "Um, no rocks. Money, pencil, some paper …"

"Give me everything you've got. I'm going to bundle it all together. The McAllisters have this minivan. It's got this alarm like you never heard. At least, it used to …" Cat's voice trailed off. There was a moment's pause, then she continued. "I'm gonna chuck the whole pile, and as soon as the alarm starts up, tell Thumper to drop out the window and run for the house. You follow. I'll be right behind. Hopefully, Dekman will take off when the whooping starts and he won't even see us. Hopefully he's alone, too. Thumper can get the back door open and we'll meet inside the house. And whatever you do, be quiet."

Runner passed along Cat's plan to Thumper. The younger boy swallowed and caught his breath but drew himself into a crouch, ready. Runner gestured for Thumper to give him the knife and string. Pulling out a stub of pencil from his back pocket, he lashed it to the knife with Thumper's twine.

He handed the bundle to Cat, raised his eyebrows. *Will this work?*

Cat nodded once. The moon dropped behind a cloud and it was like she'd blinked off. There. Not there.

A crack outside, the sound of somebody stopping abruptly, the extra quiet of waiting, breath held. Directly below the fort. Cat crept toward the window. A cool breeze had begun to blow in. The darkness mightn't last.

Runner felt the air on his hot face and closed his eyes, listening for any sound in the alley to indicate where Dekman was. When he opened his eyes, he found himself in the forest of Runnerland.

No! Not now! Please, not now! He tried to picture the slit, the seam between worlds, the knife's blade. But he was distracted by the words still carved into the sky, CROSS THE LINE.

As Runner watched, the letters tightened, condensed, re-formed. An arrow. An arrow curved across the sky where the words had hung. It pointed between two horn-shaped mountains Runner had never noticed before.

It didn't feel like an invitation. It felt like a summons.

CHAPTER FIFTEEN

Time must have passed in Runnerland during his absence, though the sky was as blue as it had ever been. The last strands of smoke had faded from the unwelcome black arrow.

Runner picked himself up from beneath a tree whose spreading branches ended in tiny yellow flowers. The way forward was a sea of mud and ash, nothing growing between him and the twin devil's-horn mountains jutting from the horizon. He was pretty sure he hadn't created those mountains: he remembered when the line between sky and land had been nothing but a gently undulating smudge.

Runner cleared his mind, shut out his doubts and fatigue, and concentrated on colours of jewels, precious metals, anything beautiful and rare: emerald grass, golden leaves, flowers in coral and ruby. He flung them as far as his eyes could carry them. There wasn't time for animals, but he paused to send a stream through the land in a slurry of silver.

"That's better," Runner said as he witnessed Runnerland spring to life. "Now, about this arrow."

He began walking, but the mountains didn't seem to draw any nearer. He broke into a jog, but they remained stubbornly distant. Runner stopped beside the river for a drink and to splash his sweaty neck. What could he do?

Scooping up a handful of water, Runner eyed it. Then he picked up a stone and hucked it across the surface, watching it skip again and again.

"It'll work," he told himself. "Just do it. No thinking."

Runner backed up twenty steps, then ran at the water, crouching low as he launched himself. *Be a stone.* He landed on the flats of his feet, water skimming underneath. He worried he'd slow and sink, but he bent his full desire on moving forward and the river rewarded him by rushing him along at impossible speeds, the banks smearing past. His feet slapped against the surface, rose and fell. The mountains seemed to speed toward him.

Peering ahead, he saw the end of the river approaching fast. Not a bend in the channel, not a dwindling, just an abrupt cutoff, like he was about to surf a waterfall, only there was no noise, nothing to explain the clean edge where the river just ... stopped.

It was the end of Runnerland. Beyond that, white. Just like those first visits. No life, no colour, nothing but that unnerving blankness. Looking at the twin mountains rearing up toward him, Runner wondered if he was being stupid. A power that could overwhelm his own mind should be approached with caution. Nah. Forget caution. "The only way to fly!" he whooped as he came down with a bump on another stretch of river, bouncing back up into the sky and further and back onto dry land. With a deep breath, he moved toward the blankness of the boundary. Another step. Another. One more. Could he do it? Should he? A step.

Nothingness.

The world just ceased. There was no dimming or fading. And without the distractions of sight and smell and touch, he could hear the thrum again, that weird buzz at the heart of this land. *These* lands, it seemed now.

He had no sensation of moving, no proof that he was making any progress, but he continued to put one foot in front of the other, arms stretched out, senses attuned to anything that might stand out from the terrible whiteness that made his heart beat too fast. There was something unnerving about entering such nothingness. It was easy to forget there was goodness in the world when the world itself no longer existed. Joy, hope. He wondered now how he'd ever found peace in this void.

But still he marched forward, and as he moved, the buzz increased. Over his shoulder, the colours and sights of Runnerland hung in the air like a window onto another dimension, like the life-giving sun burning through deadening haze.

With all his being, he yearned to turn his back on this dreadful nowhere place and return to the safety and familiarity of Runnerland. But that was an illusion too. Runnerland was no longer the safe haven he'd once assumed. If there'd been one fire, there could be another. It could turn his perfect refuge into a land of cinders and ashes. Plus, he was curious. He couldn't deny he was curious to know who had written the message: CROSS THE LINE. No, he wouldn't leave until he'd solved this. No matter what he came up against, he'd see this through. After all, he had responsibilities. To imaginary squirrels, and flowers, and the ringing bluebells. Runnerland itself needed to be looked after. Protected from this ... something. This presence.

He wasn't alone. Peering into the void, Runner could perceive the outline of a person. There was something familiar about the silhouette, the tall slouching frame, the head cocked like everything in sight was ripe for the taking but probably not worth the trouble.

Dekman.

He was just standing there, letting Runner come to him. He was wearing the same black outfit he'd worn the day he came to take Runner to be initiated. But without the sunglasses. Maybe it was the missing sunglasses that made him seem less frightening.

"Dekman! What are *you* doing here? *Are* you here?"

The older boy smiled, and instead of answering, stretched out his arm and opened his clenched fist. Resting in his palm were three sticks, slightly mashed.

"Runner." He shook his head like a parent who'd caught a child trying to pull a fast one.

"Dekman. How did you get here?"

"Same as you. Through desire. For escape. For something new. For power. You think you're the only one. You're not. There's a reason we met, Runner. A reason we found each other. Preacher Sal made me realize that. Who would have thought the old coot could actually be useful?"

Runner felt a grip of panic. He hadn't seen much of Preacher Sal in the last few weeks. He tried to remember the last time. It wasn't like Sal to keep a low profile.

"I used to watch you, you know, Runner. I'd watch you out on the sidewalk with your stupid signs and your stupid tricks to fleece the sheep. The kids were drawn to you, Runner.

They liked you. I kept asking myself, Why did they like you so much? Why did they keep pestering you, hanging around you? Asking for stuff."

Runner remembered the haircuts, the paintings, all the extra chores he'd done grudgingly. He'd never seen them for what they were: openings, offerings.

"Some of the kids at the squat decided maybe straight-edge was the answer. And we couldn't have that, now could we, Runner? We couldn't have a decline in business. Not in our own backyard."

Dekman's eyes closed for a moment, the muscles of his neck clenched as he ground his jaws. Then his eyes snapped open again and fixed on Runner. Blue flecked with silver. Just like his own.

"They kept an eye on you on the street. You probably never even noticed. What is it, Runner? Why you? I'm curious. What is it that made them all want to look out for you? To defy me?"

He licked his lips and went on. "You weren't cool. You didn't party. You never belonged. I was right that first time I ever saw you. I should have listened to myself. Slumming. You've probably got a nice mommy and daddy to run back to. But the kids stood up for you. How did you get into their heads like that, Runner? That's what I need to know. *How did you make them care about something other than their own stupid selves?"*

Runner looked at Dekman with something like pity.

"Dekman, how did you get here? How did you do it?"

"You just never understood. We're not so different, you and I. I thought maybe that's why they turned to you. They're not the brightest. Maybe they just got us confused. I watched you, Runner. I saw you out there, day after day, with your eyes closed, a little smile on your face. I wanted that smile. I wanted that peace. I wanted into your head. So I *encouraged* Preacher Sal to explain his strange little theories, the worlds without end. Drugs brought me part of the way. Desire did the rest. Almost the rest. I could never quite follow. I knew you were out there, somewhere beyond this stupid endless white. I could feel you near. I sent messages. I always sent messages, but there was something between us.

"I've run out patience, Runner." He held out the three sticks. "Recognize these? I pulled them out of a certain park." Dekman grabbed the front of Runner's coat with one arm and yanked it up under his chin.

Runner coughed against Dekman's fist. "What is it you want?"

"I want," Dekman said, throwing his other arm up into the air. "I want what you've got, Runner. I want all that," he pointed back the way Runner had come, "whatever that is.

I want the powers you have in this place and in the real world. We're not so different, so why should you have the freedom and the friends and a family? I know there's a family out there somewhere waiting for you, Runner. I can smell it on you. You're not like the rest of them. You've got a nice comfy home and rich parents out there somewhere. I want all that, and I want to cross out of this whiteness too. I'm looking for some changes."

Dekman tightened his grip on Runner's collar.

"I want to be you. And I think I know how to do it."

Runner struggled to distract the youth, to postpone whatever horrible fate Dekman had in mind. "But the fire. The smoke. You made those. How?"

"Fire," Dekman nodded bitterly. "Yeah. Fire is the one thing I *can* do here, but burning nothing is still nothing. Those mountains: fire wreathed in smoke. There's got to be more, Runner. And I'm going to have it."

Dekman shoved the sticks into Runner's face. They burst into flame, three burning caterpillars writhing in Dekman's palm.

"You get a choice, Runner," he said, jerking his chin toward his hand. "Choose your path. One of these will take you back across the line to your own land. Then you can do whatever you want. One of them will let you wake up in the real world. And one of them will let me out of this place and into your world. Into your life. Into you."

Dekman's eyes danced with a fierceness that matched the tiny fires blazing in his open hand.

Runner looked at the three tiny flames. They were identical. There was no way to choose between them. He tried to think. He remembered Cat, who burned with a frantic energy of her own. Thumper and the magic he'd learned on the street, the power to make things disappear off store shelves and reappear in his pockets. The other kids and their paranoia, their loyalty, their anger.

Another face rose up in his mind. Preacher Sal. Preacher Sal and his outlandish ideas, his fears and fancy words, his parallel universes, his heavens and hells. And his buggy. His buggy full of cardboard. Which could burn, Runner suddenly realized. A conflagration. *That's* where he'd learned the word, from Preacher Sal. That's where the cardboard must have gone. Dekman, and probably Spike, stealing all the cardboard, hoarding it in the basement for the right moment. A splash of gas and the house is history. Three storeys reduced to ash.

Three storeys, three friends who'd made it out, three flames in Dekman's hand, zigging and zagging. Three terrible beauties wriggling in his palm.

Runner spoke, unsure how much time had passed, seconds or hours. "And if I'm right, if I choose the one that lets me back across the line, we both leave, okay? We leave this place and I never want to see you again. Here or there. I don't want you messing with the other kids, either. Okay?"

A wave of pain washed across Dekman's face but the grin he gave was wolfish, eager. "Yes, Runner. That's right. All you have to do is choose. Choose right, that is. Choose right and we say bye-bye to this place. No more Dekman."

Runner felt the moment stretch and open into two moments, then four, then eight, time doubling and re-doubling into eternity. He needed to take control. Dekman was right about that. He needed to choose. But how? Runner thought of his father, his father who said that every problem has a solution so obvious it's sometimes easy to overlook it. You reduce the possibilities until only one course of action remains. His father was at the centre of this choice, Runner was sure. His easygoing father doing his best by his clients, by his family, turning chaos into order, smoothing people's lives and deaths. His father who'd taken someone else's baby and sworn a lifetime of love and care. Who'd hidden a secret, yes, but not to harm.

With a great effort, Runner pulled himself out of the hypnotic stare, reached out and closed his hand over Dekman's, pressing all three fires into the rough skin.

Runner looked into Dekman's eyes, so eerily a reflection of his own. "There are only the rules we make ourselves.

I learned that here. There are only the rules that we agree to, that we let into our lives. And I don't like your rules anymore, Dekman. I didn't like them before, but I didn't know how to stop them. Now I do. I choose no fire. I choose no pain. I choose to stay in charge of myself and my life. I don't let you in. I don't let you win."

The hum ceased as the smell of singing flesh overpowered all other senses.

Runner barely had time to get his bearings before Cat slammed into his back. He'd stopped like an idiot at the base of the tree fort's ladder and she was sliding down too fast to stop. The two of them tumbled in a knot of arms and legs. If it hadn't been for the threat of a vengeful Dekman out there in the darkness, Runner would have laughed. Instead, he picked himself up and tried to focus.

The house was sixty feet or so away. He could see Thumper up on tiptoes patting the frame above the door, searching for something, spare keys Runner guessed. Despite the ache in his chest, he ran across to the back door just as Thumper opened it, and all three stumbled across the threshold and into a laundry room. Washer, dryer, sink, damp laundry hanging from a yellow polypropylene rope strung between two corners. A towel brushed his shoulder as he turned to survey the room. It was second nature now to check every new space he entered. He wondered if that caution would ever fade.

The walls were painted a pale blue, a shade lighter than the low ceiling, which looked navy in the moonlight trickling through half-closed blinds. The effect was homey and tidy. It was nearly four months since he'd stepped into a house other than the squat, and Runner was struck by the contrast. It made him realize how dirty, how wild, he'd become. They'd all become.

He could also tell how bad they must look from the expression on the faces of the two people who appeared in the doorway and snapped on the overhead light. Busted. The elderly man, tall and thin with a shock of snowy hair swept youthfully off his forehead, showed dismay and disgust at the sight of three homeless kids panting and peeking through the curtains back out at the yard. The woman, who was the same height as Runner and apple-cheeked like a fairy-tale grandma, brought her hand up to her mouth, then let out a small shriek from behind it.

"Elizabeth! Daniel! Oh, is it really you? Here? But it's the middle of the night!"

She reached blindly for the man beside her. "Can it be? You both look starved. They look starved, don't they, Francis?"

Elizabeth? Daniel?

The man gave the briefest of nods, but his eyes were focused on their movements, Cat and Thumper still checking the backyard for signs of Dekman. He turned his attention to Runner and frowned. Runner didn't know what to do or where to look, so he studied the ceiling while he waited for someone to do something. Grey. The ceiling wasn't blue at all, but battleship grey. Despite everything, he was obviously still a chronic optimist.

"Well," the man said, clearing his throat. "We'll get the whole story, I'm sure, but let's get out of the laundry first. That is, if you and your young friend here aren't just passing through?" He eyed the door meaningfully.

Cat spoke for the three of them. "No, Grandpa. We're hoping we can stay?"

CHAPTER SIXTEEN

Peter stood at the pay phone outside the diner where he'd begun his life with the squat and Dekman and Cat and Thumper and the rest. He paused as he recalled that far-off breakfast with droplets of jam raining down all around him. Not all the memories were bad ones.

But some were. And there were still rough times ahead. This particular one might be the hardest of all. Yvonne, Cat and Thumper's grandmother, had been coaching him all morning, but he still worried he'd just lose his temper and start yelling, or bawling, or both. He was so nervous he'd come to a public phone instead of calling from Cat's.

He sucked in a breath, then set his fingers to dialing the familiar numbers.

Ellen picked up after the first ring. It was like she knew.

"Mom. It's … it's Peter."

"Peter! Oh, thank God. When I didn't hear from you—"

"Mom, I'm sorry. I never should have stopped calling like that. Without warning you. I was pretty angry …"

"Peter. I can't believe it's you. You're all right. Are you all right?"

Peter shrugged into the phone. "I'm still pissed, actually."

He waited for a reprimand for the language, but instead he heard crying.

"Mom?"

"Oh Peter, you have no idea how worried I've been. It's been five weeks since I heard from you. The last time we quarrelled and when I didn't hear, well, when I didn't hear I feared the worst."

Peter felt a lump in his own throat. He'd started in anger but in this moment he missed Ellen terribly. And Jack. He missed his father so much he could barely breathe. Every part of him ached. He blinked tears out of his eyes.

"Mom, I wanted to call sooner, but I wasn't ready. I've sorted some stuff out here. I've kinda found my feet, I guess. About Dad. And stuff."

"Oh Peter," his mother said. "I'm just so relieved to

hear your voice. The police will be relieved too. You're practically a Most Wanted right now. They took some photographs and they're everywhere — all across the country. Didn't you see them?"

Peter fed more quarters into the phone. "Mom. I'm sorry. I really am. For running away. And for not calling. Yvonne says — she's a friend — she says anger is a stage of grief just like crying and stuff. She says it's pretty normal, everything I did. Extreme, maybe."

"Peter. Come home, honey. Please. Come home."

Peter cleared his throat. This was a thousand times harder than he'd thought it would be. "Mom, I can't come home. At least not for a while. I just can't."

Ellen's voice took on an edge. "Peter. Your place is here, with me. In this house. At your school. Your friends — your real friends — keep asking about you. Mary-Beth keeps asking. I want you to come home."

Peter shook his head, like she could somehow read the gesture from that distance. "No, Mom. Not yet."

Over dinner one evening a few weeks later, Peter drew the folded, grubby envelope out of his pocket and placed it in the centre of the table. He fussed with the edges, aligning it until it sat exactly square to his placemat. He still felt shy living in this house, calling Cat and Thumper by these other names, answering to Peter instead of Runner, but every day was a little easier, as Yvonne had promised it would be. For an old woman, their grandmother seemed to understand a little of what he was going through. Which made him feel grateful. Grateful enough to help out, pull his own weight. He'd painted the garage, though he was sticking to solid colours — no cartoon horror scenes this time. And grateful enough to pay attention to their little kindnesses, like they way they didn't make a big deal about the nightmares that continued to haunt him. Dekman wreathed in clouds and smoke, flicking a lighter, blowing gasoline onto the flame like a fire eater in some dark circus. Dekman burning down houses, libraries, one time a hospital of abandoned babies. Another night a dream about Preacher Sal folded into himself like a gargoyle, perched at the bottom of a sweep of stairs, smiling to Peter from one side while Dekman casually flicked matches from the top of the staircase. Heaven and hell? Angel and devil?

Peter woke from these dreams panting and feeling lost. Yvonne got into the habit of leaving the hall light on for him, sometimes a radio downstairs. "To help you find your way back," she said one morning, the only time they discussed his troubles. Her husband still treated them guardedly — stubbornness obviously ran in the family — but he was starting to thaw.

And now Peter was grateful enough, finally, to trust this half-mended family with the envelope that had brought him so far.

Smoothing out the paper, Peter said he figured he was maybe ready to start looking for the people whose names weren't on there, his other mother and father. He'd asked Mary-Beth if she would help. She'd been onto the Internet and already found a few places to start. If she kept this up, he was going to have to get her to slow down. He needed this to unfold at his own pace. Nobody else's. Besides, he was busy. Her price was one painting of Runnerland, and Peter had begun a scene from his final visit, the beauty of everything he'd created, the arrow sinister in the distance. Or he might paint over that part. Maybe just something innocent and pure, before the fall.

He missed the place. He missed it with all his heart and soul. It was like a part of him had been cut away when he and Dekman left Runnerland. He remembered the shadow cut from the other Peter, Peter Pan, and now he knew how that must have felt. The emptiness. The loss. He felt certain that his time in Runnerland was over. It had come to him — opened within him? — at a time of need, but now he had to get by without it.

He could paint it, but a painting wasn't really a replacement. He didn't think there'd ever be a replacement for Runnerland. There would be happiness, yes. But not in that other world. Not like that.

Cat — Elizabeth — was fiddling with her noodles, rolling and unrolling them against her spoon until her grandmother gave her a cheerful swat. "Elizabeth, honey. Can't you ever sit still?"

"Not for instead," Peter said absent-mindedly, spinning the paper like a compass seeking north. He was thinking of his dad's relaxed independence, his mom's restraint, the quiet, careful house they'd brought him into. "For also."

The adults nodded, like they could follow his private reasoning, and returned to their pasta.

Peter fingered the friendship bracelet Mary-Beth had sent as a replacement. They were maybe going out, and he was working part-time at a paint store (no more fast food courts!) to pay for phone calls and computer time so they could sort out all the craziness that had happened. Plus all the questions that still lay ahead. What would happen with her Peter couldn't say, but as he surveyed the pitted landscape of his life over the past months, as his eyes lifted to take in the first blossoms pushing out new life on the tree framing the dining room window, he felt an ease. It was hard finding people; he knew the search for his birth parents wouldn't be easy. He didn't think dating by telephone was going to be a breeze either. But it couldn't be any harder than holding on to the people he already had, especially if he was going to insist on starting over in this city, so far from what he'd once called home.

His father was still in his heart, his mother too, already arm-wrestling him on the phone about when she could come out. She was so sure everything would be fine now, and Peter yearned to agree, but he had doubts. Life no longer seemed so black-and-white.

Looking around the table, though, at this temporary family he'd lucked into, Peter told himself to relax. Maybe he wasn't doing such a bad job after all. He might not have all the answers, but he was working on it. All things considered, he was probably already halfway there.

ACKNOWLEDGMENTS

I couldn't have started this book without financial support from the Canada Council for the Arts. And I couldn't have finished it without emotional support from Catherine, Rowan, and Skye, and from the rest of my family (a term I've come to appreciate for its flexibility).

This is not a book that tells you what you should do if a parent dies or you decide to run away. (It does tell you how to steal cardboard from the public library, though, which I think is a really bad idea in real life.) If you're young and looking for help and advice, there are lots of resources out there. Start with Kids Help Phone in Canada (1-800-668-6868) or Covenant House (1-800-999-9999) in the United States, and don't give up. There's someone out there who wants to help you.

JOHN BURNS is the books editor of Vancouver's *Georgia Straight* newspaper. He has contributed to the *Globe and Mail, NUVO* magazine, the *Toronto Star* and the CBC's *Arts Today*. He is also co-host of CBC Radio's Studio One Book Club, which has featured such authors as Margaret Atwood, Lemony Snicket, Kenneth Oppel and Salman Rushdie. Before publishing *Runnerland*, John co-authored a cookbook called *The Urban Picnic* (Arsenal Pulp Press, 2003). He lives in Vancouver.

By printing *Runnerland* on paper made from 100% recycled fibre (40% post-consumer) rather than virgin tree fibre, Raincoast Books has made the following ecological savings:

- 22 trees
- 1,987 kilograms of greenhouse gases (equivalent to driving an average North American car for 4.5 months)
- 16 million BTUs (equivalent to the power consumption of a North American home for two months)
- 25,040 litres of water (equivalent to nearly one Olympic sized pool)
- 745 kilograms of solid waste (equivalent to nearly one garbage truck load)

(Environmental impact estimates were made using the Environmental Defense Paper Calculator. For more information, visit http://www.papercalculator.org.)

RAINCOAST BOOKS
www.raincoast.com

ANCIENT FOREST
FRIENDLY